# SECURING THE BAG

ACE GUCCIANO

# 1

A black minivan cruised down the block at a sluggish pace then slowed a bit more as it neared the middle of the block. "Circle the block one more time and make sure ain't no police coming," said Brandon.

"Man, you sure this dude keeps his money in that raggedy ass house?" Eddy inquired. "I ain't doing this shit for nothing." He kept driving down the street as Brandon sat on the passenger side, nervously pulling on a joint.

"The dude got at least thirty or forty grand in there."

Eddy shook his head in doubt. "Why I never heard of him then?"

Brandon became frustrated with all Eddy's questions. For a second, he wished he had come alone but he was afraid of doing it by himself. "Because he's not a drug dealer," he explained "He's a goddamn jacker that runs with Spud."

"Spud?" Eddy asked with surprise. "Aw, he good to go." Eddy parked at the end of the block, and they casually strolled up to the house. "What now?"

Brandon fished a key out one of the many flowerpots that cluttered the screened-in porch and flashed it at Eddy. "I know somebody who knows somebody," Brandon bragged. Seconds later, they entered the dark living room of the house. The place reeked of cat shit and was decorated with old, worn down furniture. Photographs of older country looking white people filled the walls and mantle. Eddy couldn't believe what his eyes revealed to him.

"What the fuck is this?"

Brandon smiled as he dug a flashlight out his jacket pocket. "A cover-up, that's all. Follow me."

Eddy followed Brandon into the master bedroom. Against the far wall next to the bed was a large fish tank that housed a million rocks and a huge snake. "Just like she said," Brandon stated with a smile. He rushed over to the tank and removed the top as a black and red diamondback slithered over a small tree buried between the rocks. The sight of the snake sent a chill down Eddy's spine.

"What the fuck're you doing?" Eddy whispered loudly.

"Chill." Brandon pulled a small white mouse out his pocket and tossed him inside. As he peered over at Eddy, the snake struck the mouse. While the snake was busy feasting, Brandon reached in and took him out then placed it on the bed.

"Help me, "Brandon instructed as he started scooping out the rocks from the tank and setting them onto the floor. After the last rock was removed, they came upon a piece of cardboard so Brandon reached in and removed it. There, staring them in the face, were two layers of bundled money.

"Ooh, Brandon!" Eddy shouted. "There it is, man."

"We're only taking half," Brandon explained.

"Why half?"

"Because I know the dude. Besides, he might not trip so hard if we don't take it all." After they finished bagging the money, they replaced the rocks and snake inside the tank then left.

While Brandon and Eddy were breaking and entering, Randy and Olivia were walking out the movie theater.

"That was a good movie," Olivia commented as she wrapped her arm around him. "Thank you, baby." She sweetly said before she kissed his cheek.

"Thank me when we get home."

"I can do that, even though my lip is still a little swollen from when you slapped me the other night," she replied as she touched her lip.

Randy sighed, "Don't start. We've been having a good time."

"I know," Olivia agreed. "I'm sorry. I'll—"

"Just don't say nothing." Randy thought about the bag of money under his seat. "I got to stop and put up some money first."

"Aw, man," Olivia pouted. "I'm ready to go home so we can do our thing."

"It's not gonna take no time for me to—"

"Um hmm," she murmured with her lips turned up. Randy came to a halt next to his Chevy Blazer and kissed her. "Let's do it out here," Olivia suggested. Randy saw her nipples protruding through her blouse as he climbed into the truck, and Olivia continued to beg as she followed suit. She clutched his zipper and tugged at his pants.

"Damn, bitch, calm down," Randy angrily said. "You act like you going dick crazy."

Glaring at him, Olivia said, "That was uncalled for, Randy. You sure know how to ruin a good time." She sat with her arms folded across her chest.

"I'm sorry. C'mere." The smile she fought so hard to contain eased across her face. "I'm not fooling with you, Randy."

"A'ight."

Less than two minutes into the drive all was forgiven and Olivia's face was buried in Randy's lap. She came up for air and wiped the slob from around her mouth with her hand when she felt Randy park the truck in the driveway of his safe house. She had been giving him head the whole way there. "Hurry up, baby," Olivia said eagerly.

"Be right back." When Randy opened the front door, he didn't hear his alarm beep. He placed his hand on his gun and listened for sounds of movement. He didn't hear anything so he figured he must have forgotten to activate it. When he didn't see any signs of forced entry, he went into the bedroom and cut on the light. After he removed the cover to the tank, he peered down and saw a mouse's tail hanging out the snake's mouth. Randy reached in and removed the snake, then the rocks, and eventually the cardboard. Someone had discovered his stash spot but only half of the money was missing. Backing against the wall, he glanced around the room while clutching the butt of his gun tucked away in his jeans. After a minute or so of stillness, he didn't hear a sound so he moved towards the closet. Randy removed the sheet that covered the large birdcage hanging from the ceiling, unveiling Lemonade, his big lime green and yellow parrot. Sitting on the floor beneath it was a jar of bird-seeds. He shook a few into the palm of his hand then fed them to Lemonade.

"You hear anything good, ole buddy?" Randy asked. Lemonade wildly flapped his wings then opened his mouth.

"Occcccck! Ooh, Brandon, I knew you'd come through," Lemonade mimicked and Randy smiled.

Randy was silent when he got back in the care and he wasn't interested in Olivia finishing him off. Once they reached home, Randy paid the babysitter and sent her away. While Olivia prepared to hop in the shower, he got on the phone with an agent from the alarm company and learned his security system had been deactivated earlier that evening. He had not been there in days and there was only one other person who had the code; Olivia.

Olivia threw on her robe, picked up her towel, and walked toward the bedroom door. Soon as she crossed the threshold, her throat was seized by Randy's strong hand. She gasped as he raised the butt of his gun to strike her on her forehead.

"Ouch!" Olivia hollered as she fell onto the bed, losing the grip she had on the towel. "Owww!" She held her head in a daze, wondering what happened. As soon as her head settled, she peered up and saw Randy standing over her. His arm was wrapped around their daughter, Tiffany's, shoulder with the gun in his hand. "Call your fuckin' brother, now," Randy demanded in a calm but deadly tone. Olivia trembled under his cold stare.

"Okay. I . . . I-I." She stopped attempting to speak and picked up the phone. Brandon answered after two rings. "Brandon, what did you do? Why is—"

Randy snatched the phone from her hand with his free one as the hand that held his gun remained on Tiffany's shoulder. When

Olivia reached out for her, Randy took a step back. "Brandon," Randy spoke. "You got twenty minutes to bring me my fuckin' money or I'ma kill your sister . . . And if that don't do it, I'ma kill your niece too. You hear me?" Tiffany peered at her mother with terror-filled eyes. She was only six but could sense she was in danger.

"Man, I didn't—"

"Twenty minutes." Randy hung up as tears streamed down Olivia's face.

"You would kill me and your own daughter over some shit Brandon done? Huh?"

"Shut up, bitch. You could be in this just as deep as he is for all I know. Tell me, how did he find out where I kept my money? Or better yet, how did he deactivate the goddamn alarm?"

"I—ouch!" Olivia shrieked after Randy slapped her. She rolled off the bed onto the floor. Randy kneeled beside her and punched her in the face.

"Answer me, bitch!"

"I told him where the key was," Olivia admitted. "I turned off the alarm earlier today." She paused to sniffle. "He was just supposed to be taking some girl over there for a while, that's all." She wiped the blood from her nose. "I didn't know he—"

"You's a dumb ass bitch. You know that?" Randy kicked her in the leg.

Tiffany grabbed him. "Daddy?" she called.

"Please don't hurt my baby," Olivia murmured. Randy raised the gun toward Olivia and Tiffany gasped.

"Daddy!"

"I should kill your ass," Randy stated in a cold voice as he lowered the gun. "You'd better pray that sucka brings my money." He grabbed Tiffany and left the room.

Brandon had to break the news to Eddy that they had to return the money, but Eddy refused to hand over his half of the fifty-thousand-dollar split. He had risked his life to obtain it so it was his to keep.

"That's my big sister and my little niece," Brandon pleaded. "Please, man. We have to give it back."

"Un uh. That's your problem, dawg." Eddy grabbed his bag of money and backed toward the exit.

"Eddy, don't leave my family hanging like that."

"Trust me, dawg. He's not gonna kill his own family, he's not that crazy." Eddy opened the door. "I promise to get at him if he does you, man. I'm out."

"Please, Eddy!" Brandon begged. "I can't . . ." Eddy closed the door and left. Seconds later, Brandon heard the squeal of Eddy's tires as he pulled off. "Fuck!"

Randy was sitting on the sofa next to Tiffany when the doorbell rang. Olivia, who was sitting directly across from them, jumped up when she heard the sound.

"You want me to answer it?" Olivia asked nervously. Randy held his daughter close then nodded. Brandon immediately saw the distressed look on his sister's battered face when the door swung open. "Brandon, why?" she cried. "Why you do that?"

He tried to respond but nothing came out. Brandon stepped inside the house and faced Randy who shot daggers at him before he cocked his gun. "Gimme my fuckin' money," he growled and Brandon tossed him the bag. "Empty it." Brandon dumped its contents on the floor, twenty-five grand short. Randy could easily tell by glancing at it that it wasn't all there and raised his gun. Fear covered Brandon's face as he cringed, preparing to take the slugs Randy fired.

*Pow!*

Brandon fell back against the door, clutching his stomach. "Fuck is the rest of my money?" Randy shouted. Olivia scooped Tiffany up and hurried across the room.

Brandon spit out a clot of blood. "E—Eddy, man. He wouldn't gi-give his half back." Tears formed in his eyes.

Slowly, Randy rose from the sofa. "You knew damn well I wasn't gonna let you live, didn't you?" Brandon's eyes closed as his pain was becoming unbearable.

"W-we only took half."

"Well you should've took all of it and ran with Eddy. Now you's a dead thief."

*Pow! Pow!*

Brandon's body jerked with each blast. "Nooo!" Olivia screamed, as she shielded Tiffany's eyes from the horrific sight. "That's my baby brother!"

"Now he's your dead brother." Randy spat on Brandon's lifeless face then left the house for the last time. Fifteen minutes after Olivia called the police, and they pulled Randy's truck over.

He was arrested and charged with second-degree murder.

# 2

---

**F**ifteen Years Later...

Spud jumped on the freeway headed south in his blue BMW and the warm night's breeze swooshed in through the sunroof as he accelerated. He could see emergency lights flashing about a half mile ahead so he clutched his gun in case he had to toss it. His increasing heart rate settled after he rounded the bend and saw the cause of the flashing lights. Thankfully, they were coming from a tow truck and not the cops. The last thing Spud wanted to do was toss his gun because his head was wanted by at least ten people for a stint of robberies and homicides around town. In fact, the only reason he was still breathing was because his enemies fired on him from long distances. They lacked the courage to come within ten feet of him.

His crew of thieves consisted of five people, including himself. There was Big Boi who scouted the hits, Alvin supplied the artillery, Chuck drove the getaway car, and the beautiful Yandy was used like a delicate piece of meat, encouraging victims to bite.

Together they were responsible for ten percent of the city's murder rate. When the 55th Street exit came up, Spud got off the freeway then drove all the way to Brooklyn Avenue and made a left. As he neared the middle of the block, he slowed to a coast and picked up his cell phone.

"Hello."

"Randy, bring yo' ass outside," Spud yelled into the phone. Minutes later, Randy stepped out on the porch. Spud could see from the distance he was sporting a bald head instead of dreads and he had dropped at least fifty pounds of fat. Randy took his time finishing his cigarette before flicking it to the grass.

"See you in the morning, mama," he hollered over his shoulder as he started toward the BMW. Randy had just been released from prison hours earlier. He was the sixth member of Spud's crew before he got locked up. Honestly, he led the crew prior to his indictment in '89. Back then they were more organized. Now, under Spud's command, they were a bunch of bloodthirsty, money hungry cowboys.

"Randy!" his mother shouted. "Try not to kill nobody. You just got out."

Randy ignored his mother and got inside the comfortable interior of the BMW. "A forty-year-old mama's boy," Spud joked. Randy peered at Spud who was thirty-eight but still the size of a five foot seven thirteen-year-old boy. He was handsome and an immaculate dresser.

"You got that right," Randy retorted. "She's the only one who drove three hours to see me every month."

"Yeah, well at least I kept your books straight," Spud said in defense as he drove away.

"That you did."

"What happened to the dreadlocks?"

Randy ran his palm over his bald head. "Stress. It's a muthafucka being locked away, man."

Spud lit a cigarette. "I hope I never find out."

Randy observed the lavish leather and wood grain interior of the new car. The navigation system lit up the whole front seat. "Money must be good," Randy commented and Spud smirked.

"We done came a long way from robbing drug dealers. Now we hittin' big businesses and shit like on TV," he chuckled. While they strolled up the avenue, Randy observed the scenery like a child looking through a candy store's window. The streets had changed. The small family-owned businesses that were once around had either moved, shut down or been replaced. Wire wheels were no longer in style and fifteen-inch rims weren't even considered a big anymore. Now rims were twenty-eight inches tall, some of them even costed five figures. Now that Randy had turned forty, flashy wheels and drugs wasn't where his head was.

Randy picked up Spud's cell phone and asked, "How do you use this thing?"

"Dial the number then press send," he instructed. "Who you calling?"

"Shanara. She's at the hotel waiting on me."

"Shanara?" Spud repeated in a surprised tone. "Aw, shit, man. That skeezer was everybody's bitch while you was gone. Now she's got five kids and broken down," he laughed. "Man, you kill me."

Randy shrugged. "She kept writing letters and sending me change while I was down. Even visited once or twice. The least I could do to show gratitude is fuck her."

"I guess."

"Besides, I'm horny as a muthafucka. Do you realize I'm forty and haven't sucked a pussy?"

"Really? What about Olivia?" Randy went silent. Spud said, "Aw, man, let that shit go. Her brother stole your money, so you had to kill him. The muthafucka shouldn't have done it. I would've killed both of 'em."

"Whatever happened to Olivia?"

Spud sucked his teeth. "I don't know. Last I heard the bitch moved to Columbia."

"I missed my family."

Spud was unsympathetic. "Well obviously, they didn't miss you or the bitch wouldn't have put you away. Point blank." Spud drove Randy to the hotel on 87th Street next to the Amoco gas station. The parking lot was full. A light blue '96 Chevy Impala was parked at the entrance and Spud parked behind it. "A'ight, you old muthafucka," Spud teased.

Randy gazed at the entrance doors. "I'ma shack up here for a few days so you know where to find me if you need me."

"I'm coming in to use the bathroom." He pulled a condom out his pocket on their way inside. "Use this. Right now you're disease free. Keep it that way."

"Good lookin' out," Randy said as he accepted it. The two occupants of the Impala heard the voices and turned around. The driver winced when he saw Randy's familiar face. He had aged a little and had grown a goatee but it was him. Eddy reached inside his glove box and removed his gun.

"Wha'sup?" his friend asked with concern.

"That's that nigga that killed Brandon." The dude glanced out the back window at the two figures entering the building.

"What you wanna do?"

"I promised Brandon I would kill that nigga if something happened to him."

"Let's do it."

After Randy obtained the room key from the front desk, he and Spud found Room 205. Randy's manhood was throbbing from the excitement. He could already feel the insides of Shanara's warm pussy. "Here we go," Randy said out loud. "Room 205." He placed the key in the slot and when the light flashed green he turned the handle. "Hellooo!"

Shanara hurriedly pushed play on her portable radio then took her position on the bed with her legs open as Earth, Wind & Fire blared through the speakers. As Randy stood in front of the TV, Spud ducked into the bathroom. Randy's eyes scanned her chocolate body. Her titties were starting to sag, her belly had a small pudge, and stretch marks surrounded her waist like a belt but she was still fine in the face. There were no laugh lines or dark circles around her eyes.

Shanara cupped her sagging titties and gently massaged them while Randy forced himself not to laugh. He had gotten used to looking at the flawless young models inside the magazines in prison. However, since Shanara looked out for him, he planned on making her his main broad. He was still going to find a young, tender mistress to fuck though. Spud snuck out the bathroom, hit Randy with a smile, then crept out the door. As Randy approached the bed, Shanara got on her knees and started tracing his muscular arms with her hands.

"I see you made good use of all that time," she complimented, referring to his muscles. Instead of replying, he kissed her and Shanara immediately began undressing him.

When Spud walked out the hotel room, Eddy and his partner were strolling up the hallway. Eddy's buddy nodded at Spud, but Spud being the hard gangsta he was, ignored him and kept on walking. Eddy and his friend lingered in the hallway until Spud disappeared around the corner.

"Which room did he come out of?"

"This one here," Eddy replied as he took out his gun and knocked on the door.

Randy was lying in bed with Shanara on top of him as he gently caressed her back while she nibbled on his neck and face. He slid his hands down to her butt cheeks, guiding her up and down on his dick.

"Yessss," Shanara murmured. "Give it to me, old man."

*Knock. Knock.*

Shanara frowned as she turned her head toward the door. "Who in the hell—" The sudden jerking feeling inside her womb alerted her that Randy was cumming. "I know you didn't cum."

Randy grinned bashfully. "I did just get out after doing fifteen years without pussy. You should be proud your pussy is so good."

Shanara scowled. "Proud? Nigga, I'm mad I didn't get mine."

"I'm not through, just give me a second to rest up. Now go get the door."

She stared at him for a moment. "It better get back up." She kissed his lips then got up. He watched her put on her blouse and head for the door. Her unbelievably still firm ass jiggled as she walked.

"You still got a trunk on that old Buick," he joked. She smacked one of her cheeks and kept walking. Randy rose from the bed and walked into the bathroom. When Shanara opened the door, Eddy had the gun pointed at her face and a wave of horror fell over her. Standing before the mirror, Randy gazed down at his limp organ. He noticed when hard it didn't stand as straight as it used to when he was twenty-five. Now it was tilted a little to the right.

"Baby," Shanara called in a weak voice. Randy could tell by her voice there was trouble. He stepped to the side of the closed bathroom door.

"Yes?" he answered.

"Nobody was at the door," she lied. "Come out so we can finish." Her voice was shaky.

"I'm 'bout to take a shower."

"I'm coming in." The door slowly eased open as Randy stood behind it. Through the crack he saw Shanara walk in with Eddy behind her, holding his gun in her back. Randy waited until he thought she was safely through then kicked the door closed on Eddy's hand with all the force he could muster but not before Eddy fired a single round into Shanara's back.

She fell forward onto the sink, but Randy didn't have time to check on her. His own life was on the line. The door slammed on Eddy's arm again as another shot fired into the wall. Randy kicked the door repeatedly until the gun fell to the floor. When he reached down to get it, the door flung open and he was knocked on his side. Eddy rushed in holding his right arm and kicked him. Spud barged in the room just as Eddy's friend entered the bathroom.

*Pow! Pow!*

Spud fired two shots into his back and his body flew into Eddy, knocking him over Randy. Randy grabbed Eddy's sore arm and twisted it.

"Ahh!" Eddy yelled. Spud casually walked over and fired a single round into Eddy's head. Randy closed his eyes until it was over. When he felt Eddy's body jerk then go limp, he kicked him off then hurried to his feet. Shanara was lying on her back, gasping for air. Blood was all over the floor and Randy almost slipped trying to get to her.

"Call an ambulance!" Randy shouted but Spud didn't move. He had shot enough people to know that Shanara wouldn't make it.

"Randy," Spud said, "let's go, man."

"No!" Randy protested as he held Shanara's head in his arms. She gazed up at him briefly then slipped into the world of the unknown. "Spud, call the—"

"She's gone, Randy." Spud looked up when he heard the police sirens. "Let's beat it, man."

"I'm not running. I'll be here with a story to tell 'em."

"Suit yourself, just keep my name out of it." Spud left back out the way he came. Randy gazed into Shanara's dead orbs wondering why this had to happen. She looked after him while he was down and out. Now he would never get the chance to repay her. When the newspaper came out the following day, the front-page article read:

Three Killed in Hotel Room

*Two gunmen allegedly barged inside a couple's hotel room in an attempt to flee another gunman. An altercation broke out between one of the gunmen and the male hotel room occupant. During their scuffle, the gunman's firearm discharged and the female occupant was shot in the back. The third gunman was able to track them by the sound of gunfire. Entering the room, he shot the two gunmen in hiding then fled the scene while the male victim watched his girlfriend die in his arms. The survivor is listed as forty-year-old Randy Harris.*

# 3

T *wo Months Later . . .*

Ever since the triple homicide at the hotel, business had declined. Guests complained the place lacked security and the rooms weren't safe enough for the cost. All because a group of black men decided to use the place as a shooting gallery. Considering the large monthly overhead, lowering the room rates was not an option. Mr. Mike Morgen, the hotel's owner, owned many businesses in the state of Missouri. He used his street smarts and connects to help muscle small businesses into selling their companies to him and all kinds of other mischief.

His only weakness was he loved black pussy. Morgen figured most black women came from poor backgrounds or were down on their luck so he showered them with expensive gifts, trips, and often bragged about his business ventures while lying in bed. But after it was all said and done, Morgen was a lonely old man. He had spent the better part of his life chasing young girls and forgot to settle with someone he could grow old with.

Someone who would love him and not his huge bankroll. He knew that the young broads only went for him because he was rich. That was why he had developed a soft spot for Yandy. Yandy pretended to love him with the skill of an old prostitute. She looked him in the eyes while he talked, tended to his needs when he was sick, and never asked for anything that wasn't forced upon her. She tried to get pregnant by him but old Morgen never laid her without protection. She even offered to be his wife which he regretfully declined. No one would inherit a dime of his fortune when he passed. He planned on spending what he could while he was alive. The rest would be donated to various charities and foundations across the world.

Morgen finished cleaning his dentures inside the bathroom of his downtown loft as Yandy was sprawled over the bed watching TV. They had just finished role playing a little while before so she wore nothing but a pair of pink lace panties and stilettos as she ran her long fingers through her bushy, goldish-brown hair. She was mixed but had more white features than black with a pointed nose and thin lips. She was long in the legs and round in the chest.

"Ready for bed, big daddy?" Yandy purred.

"Yeah. Fix me a drink first, would ya?"

"Sure." While she prepared his nightcap, he removed his silk robe, unveiling his pudgy, hairy stomach then sat on the bed. Yandy returned a minute later with his drink. "Here you go, sweetie." She climbed in bed behind him and massaged his shoulders. "You're tense. What's eating you?"

Morgen took a sip. "Business ain't so good."

"Which one? You own twenty of them."

"My hotel here in the city." He sipped on his drink. "It's been going downhill fast since those murders happened." He rubbed his sagging chin as if in thought. "I need to sell it fast before I'm forced to close it."

"Don't worry, you'll think of something." She tapped his shoulder.

"C'mon and lay down. Rest your bones." Morgen finished his drink before getting under the covers with her.

"Yeah," Morgen said. "I'll think of something. Listen, you keep your ear to the street for any potential buyers, okay? Things might get a little grimy, you know what I mean?" Yandy didn't answer but she was in deep thought. He had just given her an idea. She would run it by Spud in the morning to see what he thought.

When Spud and Yandy arrived at Laura's Soul Food diner on 75th, Randy was already sitting at a table enjoying a fried catfish dinner and watching the basketball game. The place was empty except for him and the two owners.

"Duncan can't play for shit," Randy blurted out. "All that fuckin' money he makes and he can't even make a fuckin' free throw." The cook, Terry, who was also one of the owners sat next to him shaking his head in agreement.

"Hey, Terry. What's up?" Spud said. Anybody looking could see the pistol bulging out Spud's waist. Randy shot Terry a look that said 'get somewhere'.

"Good seein' you, Spud," Terry said on his way to the back. Yandy gave Randy a hug and a quick peck on the lips.

"Mm, I've been waiting years to kiss those big, juicy lips," Yandy joked. She could see fuzz growing on his head around a bald spot. "What's up with the head?"

"Losing my damn hair."

"It's sexy."

"Quit playing," Spud interrupted as he and Yandy took a seat at the table.

"So?" Randy inquired. "What's this all about?"

Yandy decided to do the talking. "Well, a friend of mine owns the hotel that Shanara was killed at. Problem is, since the murders happened, business hasn't been good. In fact, it's looking to shut down within the next year . . ." Randy shrugged while he continued to devour his meal. "Spud and I think it would be a good idea if the crew bought it. We figured since you're the one with the brains and degree, you'd be in charge of it. You could act as manager but the six of us will split the proceeds."

Randy spit out a chicken bone. "Doesn't sound very profitable, not with six people going in on a hotel that's foreclosing."

"Exactly, Randy, but we'll be able to clean the dirty money that we be stealing," Spud joined the conversation.

"That doesn't do me any good."

"Sure, it does. You'd get to keep fifty percent while the rest of us get ten apiece."

Randy rubbed his chin as if in thought. "And I'd have total control?"

Yandy thumped her cigarette ashes in the tray. "Consider it yours."

"How much does the hotel cost?"

"Three million," Spud said as if it were a small amount.

"Y'all already got the cash?"

"Not yet, but we're working on it."

"Working on it, meaning you're planning a big score?" Randy asked and Yandy nodded. "I want in."

"Why?" Spud was curious.

"Because not only do I want to run the business, I also want part ownership. We do it my way or I won't get involved. Point blank." Yandy shifted her gaze over to Spud and smiled.

"You got it," she answered before standing and motioning for Stud to follow. "I'll be in touch." Outside the restaurant, Yandy waited at the passenger door for Spud to unlock the car. "You owe me a hundred bucks," she said across the hood of the car. "I told you he would come along."

"Yeah, yeah. Get in the fuckin' car."

Two days later Randy sat at the same table inside Laura's Soul Food joint playing dominoes with Terry. He slammed a bone down on the table.

*Blam!*

"Fifteen!" he shouted. "And domino! Shake that shit up," Randy heckled.

"You ain't gon' win if that's what you're thinking," Terry bellowed. "I betcha that!"

"If you trick 'em, you can beat 'em, Terry," Randy joked as he selected seven new bones. "Let's see here."

Yandy walked through the door in high heels, capri jeans, and a sleeveless blouse that fastened around her thin neck. Her bare chest hid behind the thin material.

"Goddamn, baby," Terry exclaimed. "You know your meal is on the house."

Yandy smiled. "Thanks, baby, but I don't do meat."

"None?"

"I take that back," Yandy peered over at Randy. "There is one T-bone cooked well done I would love to feast on."

"Ooh wee! What we gonna do with her, Randy?"

"Put her on tape and sell it in the back of a magazine." They all laughed.

Yandy said, "Seriously, Randy, I need you to take a ride with me."

Randy sucked his teeth. "Is it business or pleasure?"

"Umm, maybe a little of both." She flashed her wide grin, and Randy stood up.

"Terry, hold it down until I return."

Yandy ordered Randy to drive her Lexus truck while she rode shotgun then instructed him to take Highway 71 all the way down-town. He was relaxing to the Isley Brothers CD when she leaned over and began unzipping his pants.

"Yandy, what—"

"Relax, nigga. I'm trying to see something." Yandy opened his pants and took out his dick. She put it up under her nose and then sniffed. "Just like I thought. You ain't had no pussy, have you?" She shook his dick while talking to him. "Have you?"

"I haven't had time," he replied sheepishly. "I've been so stressed about money that it probably won't—Mmm." Randy felt her warm jaws and smooth lips as she took him in and out her mouth. Yandy positioned herself so she could go all the way down on him, feeling his head bumping her throat.

*Slurrrp! . . . Slurrrp!*

She took one of his hands and placed it on her ass. He heard her mumble about staying focused with a mouth full of saliva.

"I'm not gon' wreck your truck but . . . goddamn, this shit feels good." He swerved a little bit but immediately regained control. There was a slippery sucking noise when she quickly pulled him out her mouth.

"Man—Girl, just keep on going." He pushed her head back down.

"Stick your finger in my butt while I'm doing it."

By the time they arrived at Morgen's downtown office, Randy felt like he had actually fucked Yandy. Truthfully, he was in shock. Never had she so boldly thrown herself on him like that. Randy pulled into the parking lot.

"What now?"

She fixed her hair and lipstick inside the mirror. "Now we go in." She faced Randy. "How do I look?"

"Like a white girl."

"Good, let's go." A sexy, young black secretary about twenty-two years old escorted them to Morgen's office. He was standing by the window peering through a huge telescope at the downtown area. Randy could see gray, wavy hair that only grew on the back of his head.

Randy leaned toward Yandy and whispered, "I see we got some-thing in common."

"Shhh!" she murmured. "Baby." Morgen stopped peeping and turned around as Yandy walked to him and gave him a short but passionate kiss on the lips.

"That's enough," Morgen joked. "There's no telling where those lips have been. Huh? Huh?" he laughed and Randy laughed with him.

"Ha, ha," Yandy retorted. "Fuck both of y'all."

"So . . ." Morgen patted his stomach. "Who do we have here?"

"Mike, this is my longtime friend, Randy." She grabbed Randy's hand and pulled him to Morgen. "Randy, this is Mike." They shook hands and nodded at one another.

"Have a seat," Morgen offered as he walked behind his desk. "Can Yandy get you anything? A cigar perhaps?"

"I'm fine."

"I'll have a cigarette," Yandy said. She fired one up then took a seat next to Randy with her legs crossed and Morgen sat back in his chair.

"Randy, let me be frank and tell you I have a problem that I need you to help me solve. I own three banks. One in Springfield, another in Jefferson City, and the last here in Kansas City." Randy sat back in his chair and braced himself for what was next to come. Morgen sighed before he continued. "I want you to rob all three of them." Randy attempted to speak, but Morgen raised his hand. "Hear me out first. I'll supply you with all the inside information you'll need to carry this thing out. In the end, if it all goes well, you should make out with two million in cash and two million worth of bonds. I'll be happy to buy back the bonds at half price. Plus, I get a fourth of the two million. The money you'll get will be used to buy my hotel since I hear you took part in helping it go under anyway."

"Let me get this straight." Randy sat up. "I—we steal your money, give you a cut, then buy your unprofitable hotel? And then you'll file a claim to get your money back from your insurance company?"

"Yes," Morgen replied frankly. "That's my plan."

Randy shifted his gaze over to Yandy who winked at him. "If you say so," Randy finally agreed.

Morgen smiled. "Good. My people will be in touch with you soon." He extended his hand and Randy shook it.

Inside the dining room of Spud's home, Big Boi, Yandy, Alvin, and Chuck gathered around a round as Spud busied himself with fixing a drink. The men were dressed in black suits and mock neck shirts while Yandy had on a black suit with a white blouse. Eight minutes later Randy entered the room wearing the same suit as the others except he wore a turtleneck underneath. In his hand he carried a black briefcase that he placed on the table. He opened it, took out some slides, and tossed them to Yandy.

"Handle those for me, please," Randy commanded. While Yandy pulled down the projection screen and loaded the projector, Randy addressed the group. "How is everybody?" They all nodded. Each of them were either sipping coffee or puffing on a Newport. "First off, people, we got three banks on our list. The first is located in Springfield, the second in Jefferson City, and the last, which will be our biggest challenge, is right here in this city. The only good thing about that is Big Boi put together a good escape plan so it shouldn't be a problem." Yandy worked the controls to display the exit strategy. There wasn't a weak link in the room, and Randy was aware of that. Trust was not an issue with them. The issue was getting the jobs done and returning safely with the money.

Though Randy hadn't pulled a robbery in fifteen years and recently turned forty, Spud still felt at ease letting him come along because he remembered how well Randy handled himself at the hotel the night Eddy tried to kill him. After all the slides were shown and Randy had run out of things to say, Spud added his own afterthought.

"The most important thing," Spud said, "is that each of you know your role. Three minutes is all we have to get in and out of a bank, y'all know that." He peered at Chuck. "Chuck, what do you do if you spot the heat?"

"Get on my radio and yell abort."

"If you hear abort, drop whatever you're doing and get the hell out of there," Spud stated. "No ifs, ands or buts."

Randy scanned the well-groomed group with his hawk eyes and was impressed by what he saw. "Get out of here," he commanded. "This meeting is adjourned."

"And no fucking," Yandy added in a motherly tone. "Y'all know how pussy slows you down."

Alvin turned around pouting. "Aw, come on, ma."

"Especially not you, Alvin," Yandy said. "You act like you can't function after you get a shot of young pussy, and we don't need anybody arriving late. A late nigga—"

"Is a dead nigga," Alvin finished her statement. "I know." Everybody in the room understood that the queen meant business. Their bills getting paid depended on each of them carrying out their jobs correctly.

"Ah! Ahhh! Ahhh!" Yandy screamed in passion. She was in the doggy style position while Randy stood behind her, pounding his hammer into her backside. He grabbed her hair as she tried to scoot away from him toward the headboard. He put his knees on the bed, chasing the cat while continuously stabbing her guts. "Ooh! Ooh! Ooh! Randy, p-please. Ughhh! I promise I won't . . . Urrrgh!"

"Un uh, bitch. Don't run . . . Don't run, take it . . . Take it!" Randy grunted as his grip on her hair tightened. Yandy held onto the headboard as her body convulsed.

"I'm about to-to . . . cum!" Pussy juice squirted out her onto his dick and pelvis.

"Shiiit!" Randy panted before falling next to her on the bed. Yandy crawled on top of him, and he could feel her heart thumping against his chest. "Say you give, bitch. Callin' me a fuckin' old man."

"I give. I give, baby," Yandy surrendered as she placed her hand on her stomach. "Man, I can still feel you inside of there. I probably got bruises on my uterus."

"I was trying to kill you."

"Okay, killer." She kissed his chest then reached for her cigarettes on the nightstand. She fired up two and placed one between Randy's lips. "It's been a while. You're sure you're up for a gun fight?"

"Yeah. I had one the first day I got out, remember? A killer never loses his touch." Yandy held her cigarette away from her face while she admired him.

"I love you, Randy."

He ran his hand up her thigh. "I love you too, but we can never be together. Friends are friends so let's keep it that way."

Yandy's face reddened. "If you say so." She glanced at her watch. "I've gotta take a shower so I can leave. You're welcome to stay."

"Where you headed? To the old man's?"

"Yes." She puffed on her cigarette. "I like to be at his house when he returns, makes him feel wanted. Is there anything I can have him get you?" Randy placed his hands behind his head and locked his fingers.

"Nah, I'll have everything I need in less than a year." Yandy stood and put on a sheer robe. Her nipples stabbed at the fabric, and Randy stared at her hairy pubic mound with a lustful gaze. "Your hair is tangled," he informed her.

Yandy scratched her pelvis. "Better?" She struck a pose and he nodded in approval. "Okay." She headed for the bathroom. "I don't know why you're commenting on a pussy you don't want." Randy smiled as he shook his head.

**4**

---

R andy chose to do hit the bank in Springfield on a Wednesday because it was unlikely to be busy. Without being noticed, he headed to the men's bathroom as Yandy was inside the bank discussing a loan with the bank's manager. She was dressed in a beige business suit, low-heeled pumps, and glasses. Her hair was in a ponytail and she clutched a crocodile briefcase. Very discreetly, she took in the scenery around her while conversing with the manager.

There were four bank tellers behind the counters. Two of them in their mid-forties while the other two looked to be in their early twenties. An old guard with a gray handlebar mustache stood by the restroom door, sipping on a cup of hot java while chatting with one of the loan officers as four customers were standing in line, three women and a man. Yandy excused herself so she could use the restroom. She waited around in front of the restroom mirror and pretended to check her make-up until the bathroom cleared. Her super dark foundation, false eyelashes, and green contact lenses made her unrecognizable to even her own mother. Once the bathroom cleared, she shut and secured the door then took her radio out her bag.

"C2 to C1, over," she whispered. Chuck, Spud, and Big Boi had just pulled in front of the building in an old-school Impala when Big Boi raised his radio to his lips.

"C1 to C2. Go 'head, over." Yandy quickly gave them a description of what was going on inside the bank. The entire crew listened intently until she finished talking.

Big Boi said, "Okay, C2, we're comin' in. C1 to the road runner, get ready to move in. Over." Randy flushed the toilet inside the bank's restroom where he'd been waiting to receive the signal then checked the chamber of the P89 that Morgen had stashed behind the toilet. Dressed in black slacks and a turtleneck, he exited the stall and pulled the ski mask down over his face. Before he walked out the door, he took a deep breath. The old guard was standing right outside the door, still chatting with the female loan officer. Her blue eyes expanded in fear when she saw Randy sneak behind the old man and forcefully struck him over the head with the butt of the gun.

*Thump!*

He snatched the loan officer at the same time Alvin, Big Boi, and Spud stormed in with AK-47s. Spud held two but handed one to Randy who tucked the P89 inside his waist. "Come with me," Randy ordered the loan officer.

"Ow!" she yelped as he yanked her.

Spud shouted, "Everybody down, now! This is a muthafuckin' robbery. Do as the fuck I say and you won't be fuckin' hurt." Big Boi and Alvin rushed the four tellers with their guns drawn.

Alvin tossed the bags to Big Boi who threw them at the first teller. "Take one and pass the rest," he commanded. The bank manager froze as he watched Randy, gun in hand, dragging the loan officer his way. The guard attempted to rise, but Spud kicked him in the face then relieved him of his revolver.

Randy shoved the loan officer into the manager. "What's your name?" he yelled.

"Huh?" the loan officer replied nervously.

"Your fuckin' name! Tell me your name."

"Silvia. Silvia Clemons."

"Okay, Silvia. Tell your boss to give you the key, now." The manager's hand shook violently as he went into his desk drawer and produced a gold key. Randy snatched it from him then backhanded him with his gloved fist. Light cries and sniffles could be heard while Randy hauled Silvia across the floor and inside the vault. He took a laundry bag out his pocket and threw it at her. "Fill it," Randy ordered. "You got forty-five seconds. Keep a stack for yourself."

One of the older tellers prepared to hit the silent alarm but just to be safe she peeped above the counter to see if anyone was watching her. Over by the women's restroom, she saw Yandy peeking out the door. Yandy raised her cell phone and indicated that she had called 911 so the teller nodded then continued filling the bag. Two minutes and forty-two seconds after they entered the bank, the four men walked out the front door, each carrying a duffle bag full of money as Chuck pulled up out front in the Impala. Yandy waited until they were leaving to call the police as a frantic hostage in an active bank robbery.

Early the next morning, they drove to Jefferson City and robbed the bank that afternoon. The bank in Kansas City would be more difficult. They needed a week to recuperate before they took on that challenge. During that time, Randy made plans for his new hotel. Since the place was already downhill, he had to think of something that would bring clientele back. Something that would generate more income than any hotel in the city, enough to make him a known name across America. He wanted tickets to golf tournaments, box seats at the stadium, and to befriend famous entertainers. To sum it all up, he wanted to conquer the American dream. He wanted to be rich.

Alvin jumped out of bed as the alarm clock beeped. "What time is it?" He rubbed his eyes and turned to the nightstand. The digital clock read 3:30 p.m. in neon green light. "Oh, shit!" He jumped up and hurried into his clothes as the girl sleeping next to him raised her head from under the covers. She ran her fingers through her wild hair and let out a long sigh.

"Baby, where are you goin' now?" she inquired.

"Shut up!" Alvin hollered. "You're the fuckin' reason I'ma be late." She shot him an angry look then shook her head as she watched him run around. He couldn't find his shirt. She could tell what he was looking for by the way he was patting his chest. To assist him, she raised her naked body up and walked to the bathroom. Seconds later she returned carrying his shirt.

"Lookin' for this?" She held it up with a smile on her face, thinking she had just pleased him.

Alvin scowled. "Bitch, you find something funny?" He crept over to her and clutched her arms. "Huh?" Quickly, he released her right arm and slapped her then violently shook her.

"Baby, please," she cried. He shoved her down on the bed. Only halfway dressed, he picked up his gun and made for the door.

"And don't call me either, you funky ass whore." The woman waited until Alvin slammed the door to lift her middle finger in response.

"Fuck you," she said to the closed door.

Chuck, Spud, and Big Boi were waiting outside Alvin's house in the Impala. They had been waiting for over thirty minutes, and Spud's temperature continuously elevated as the time passed. He had become tired of glancing at his watch ten minutes before.

Big Boi looked at his. "Where's this nigga—" Before he finished his sentence, he saw Alvin's Suburban flying up the block. He whipped into the driveway and was out of the truck in a hurry.

Spud said, "Nobody say a word when he gets in here."

Alvin climbed into the backseat. "Man, I had to—" Chuck bolted away from the curb.

*Eerrrrrk!*

The bank was unbelievably crowded when they arrived. The fact that it was near closing didn't make a difference like Randy expected but the robbery still had to be carried out. Yandy walked in dressed in her usual garb and scanned the room through her dark glasses. Cameras were on every wall and above every counter but those wouldn't be a problem since the bank's owner was in on the job. There was a line of people at the ATM machine and at each of the five teller windows. There were even a few people standing in the commercial account line.

This time the security guard looked to be in his twenties and in good shape. He casually walked around tapping a flashlight against his thigh. He seemed anxious, like he was waiting on something to kick off. Yandy discreetly walked to the restroom and ducked into a stall. She texted Spud and Randy all the information they needed. Since the place was so crowded, Yandy herself would have to get involved.

She left the restroom and stood in line for teller number three.

"Hi," she heard a child's voice say. Yandy peered down and saw a little white girl staring up at her.

She put on a false smile. "Hello."

"My stepdaddy is a cop," the girl stated.

"Is that so?"

"Um hm." She pointed to a black man with a clean cut and a goatee. He was standing at the counter filling out a deposit slip. "There he is right there. He's the best . . ." The little girl's voice faded as Yandy lowered her glasses and watched the man closely. His backup revolver was bulging out of his tightfitting rugby shirt. How could she have missed something as crucial as that? The man's face had cop written all over it. That wasn't the kind of thing that she would have missed five years ago but age did have its downfalls. She looked at her watch and saw that it was almost showtime.

*Damn! Too late to call it off* she thought. Yandy would just have to play it by ear.

"Him and my mommy are getting married soon," the little girl's voice sung. "Did you hear me?"

"Huh? Yes, yes, I heard you," Yandy flatly answered before she walked away. She didn't see the little girl stick out her tongue at her. As she neared the cop, she could tell he was having a difficult time filling out the deposit slip. Yandy snuck up behind him and counted he was already on his third one. He glanced back at her and smiled then continued with what he was doing. Yandy watched him mess up another slip before offering her assistance. "Excuse me," she said, lightly tapping his shoulder, causing him to turn around. "Do you need some assistance?"

Randy hung up the pay phone outside the bank after he saw the Impala drop off its occupants. The people moving about around the area were too busy doing their own thing to notice three armed men walking inside. If they had, they probably wouldn't have believed what they were seeing. They were ten feet away from the entrance when Randy slipped in ahead of them. The security guard was at the entrance just about to start locking the doors.

"Excuse me, sir. We're closing." The security guard held up his hand.

"Ah, can't you just . . ." Randy hit him with his taser. "Make an exception?" The guard collapsed onto the floor. Spud passed Randy an AK-47 on his way over to the tellers. One of the tellers tensed when she saw Spud storming toward her with a rifle in hand. She went for the emergency button as he pointed the rifle at the center of her forehead.

"Remove your finger from that button," he commanded. The crowd turned around at the sound of Spud's voice and seeing the powerful rifle in his hands sent them into panic.

"Ahhh!" Screams came from all directions. Big Boi took one side, Alvin took the other, and Spud jumped on the counter.

"Everybody, on the floor. Now!" Randy shouted as he walked

through brandishing his weapon. The people did as they were told, but they weren't moving fast enough. Randy snatched up the policeman's little girl. "Do it now or she gets it."

Spud handed the bags to the tellers. "Fill 'em. And no funny money." The cop hesitated as he slowly got down on the floor. Yandy waited for him to comply before she dropped. She kept one hand above her head and one on the .38 inside her blazer pocket. The manager stood silent, hoping that the robber would go on without bothering him. He almost shitted on himself when he saw Randy storming toward him.

"You!" Randy yelled, pointing a stiff finger at the manager. "Come with me." He snatched the man by the collar and dragged him to the vault.

"Wh-what are you looking for?"

"Bonds," Randy replied. "All of 'em." The manager's hands shook while he opened the safe then he took a step back. "On your knees and lock your hands behind your head." After the manager obeyed his command, Randy put the AK around his neck and started filling the bags. The police officer felt helpless lying there, watching his scared stepdaughter. She was facing the wall with her hands up, having a hard time counting backward from one hundred. Randy told her if she reached one before they left she'd cheated and would be punished. After the tellers filled the bags, they handed them to Spud. He threw two of the bags at Big Boi who in turn slung one to Alvin. The cop on the floor thought that it was the perfect time to make his move. He gazed at his partner, Officer Blackberry, who was on the floor near the teller counter staring back at him. He gave Blackberry the signal to make his move. Blackberry jumped and drew his .38 revolver.

"Police! Nobody move!" he ordered with his aim at Spud. The officer next to Yandy got on his feet and drew his gun as well.

"Drop 'em now!" Alvin moved so Officer Blackberry redirected his aim from Spud and shot at him.

*Pop! Pop!*

Alvin dove behind the counter. By the time Blackberry swung his gun back to Spud, Spud had the rifle pointed at him. Just as Spud was about to shoot, the officer near Yandy fired, hitting him in the arm. When the cop took another step, he felt the barrel of Yandy's Glock buried in the small of his back.

*Pow! Pow!*

The hostages screamed as they jumped up and ran around. The little girl tightly closed her eyes and kept on counting. No one attempted to rescue her. Big Boi ran to check on Alvin as Blackberry ducked behind the manager's desk.

Inside the safe, Randy immediately stopped bagging after hearing the gunfire. Then he heard Yandy scream, "Abort!" over the radio. He zipped the bags and peeped out the safe's door. He saw Blackberry crouched behind a desk with a gun in his hand, speaking into a radio. Across the room, Yandy crouched low and fired two shots in his direction but missed.

Spud got off the floor with his sleeve soaked in blood. Big Boi and Alvin were hiding behind two pillars but sirens could be heard nearby. Randy leveled his AK at Blackberry's head.

*Du-Du-Du-Du!*

The bullets ripped through Blackberry's chin, neck, and upper chest and the radio fell from his hand. Randy walked closer to him and pointed the rifle.

*Du-Du-Du!*

Randy tossed Yandy one of the bags. "Let's go!" A blue unmarked Crown Victoria pulled in front just as they were exiting. Before the detectives got a chance to do anything, Randy and Spud fired on the car. The hail of bullets ripped through the metal like it was cotton, and the detectives inside fell to the floor for cover.

"C'mon!" Yandy yelled. She took off toward the back of the building with her adrenaline was pumping. She had never come this close to being caught before. Another car pulled up and tried to cut them off. The driver jumped out, using his door as a shield then pointed his weapon.

"Freeze!" he commanded. Yandy pointed her pistol and fired at the door's window. The officer fell backward as the bullet shattered the glass and pierced his chest.

"Go! Go! Go!" Randy yelled as shots rung from behind them. They ducked behind Popeye's Chicken and ran until they came upon a manhole. Randy stood guard until everybody was down the hole then he climbed below and replaced the lid.

"Run!" Yandy urged. Funky sewage water splashed up the legs of their pants as they ran through the dark tunnel. No one could see but they knew the direction in which they were headed.

"I can't see," Alvin whined.

"Shut up and c'mon!" Yandy yelled back at him. "Damnit!" she exclaimed as the heel of her shoe broke, causing her to fall. Randy ran to her and felt around until he found her foot then took off her other shoe.

"I got too much baggage to carry you," he said. "Get up and run barefoot. C'mon, it's just water." He helped her up and they were on the move again. They ran for several long blocks until they came upon the opening they were looking for. The Impala's powerful engine could be heard roaring and that eased their nerves a little. Chuck saw all the police riding and a helicopter patrolling the area. He was too far from the bank to see what was going on but he had heard the gunshots. His first mind told him to get ghost, but somehow, he knew they would make it out; as long as they made it to the sewer.

Seconds later he heard the doors opening and felt the car jerk as bodies fell inside. Alvin and Big Boi hid inside the trunk, Randy laid across the backseat as Spud hid on the floor, and Yandy sat in the front seat with her head between her legs. Chuck was driving up Paseo Boulevard when a policeman pulled up beside him with his wide nose all in his car. Chuck shot him an angry stare, and the policeman looked away as he sped off with his lights flashing.

Alvin and Big Boi felt the car finally come to a stop thirty minutes later. The car rocked slightly as the occupants exited before light shone inside the trunk. Yandy reached in and helped Big Boi out.

Alvin lifted his head as he waited to follow Big Boi, but Spud placed both hands on the trunk then brought it down hard on Alvin's head.

*Thunk!*

Alvin screamed but Spud lifted the trunk and brought it down again.

*Thunk!*

Then again and again. When Spud lifted the lid, he peered down at Alvin holding his bleeding head. Yandy glared down at him with her gun held tight in her hand. *Pussy has always been his downfall* she thought to herself just before she fired three slugs into his body then tossed the car keys to Big Boi.

"Get rid of it."

## 5

R andy and Yandy sat on her living room floor for hours, tallying the score with two money counters and two notepads. They took several breaks before finally finishing early the next morning. Randy sat front of the sofa wearing a white wife beater and pajama bottoms as Yandy returned from the kitchen carrying a plate of eggs and bacon.

"Breakfast," Yandy announced in a cheerful tone while holding the plate under his nose. Randy stared at the plate like it had a dead rat on it.

"That's not turkey bacon," he commented.

She looked at the bacon. "I know, it's pig bacon."

Randy sighed briefly. "Baby, c'mon. You know after a black man gets out of the joint there's one rule he sticks to."

"And that is?"

"Eating pork is a no-no. Now take that funky ass shit on somewhere else."

Yandy sat down Indian style next to him. "I'll eat it if you won't. My mama's sixty-eight and been eating pork all her life."

"It's a filthy animal."

"So are catfish and chicken, but I bet you eat that." Randy refused to respond because she was correct. In fact, he really couldn't give her a good reason as to why he didn't eat pork. He just knew that most incarcerated black men didn't eat it.

"Shut up," he said.

"That's what I thought. You jailbirds kill me." She chewed on the bacon. "So . . . how much did we come up with?"

Randy fired up a cigarette. "Ah . . . Three million and eight hundred thousand in cash and a million and a half in bonds. Minus that ten thousand we already gave the boys."

Yandy whistled. "Looks like we'll have a little over a million to split after we buy the hotel and pay Morgen."

Randy shook his head. "I'm keeping the extra."

Yandy stopped chewing and swallowed hard. "What do you mean by keeping the extra?"

Randy hit his cigarette before stubbing it out in the ashtray. "Just what I said. I got big plans for my hotel and I need that money to spread around. Rub elbows with some rich people who'll spend big money. I'm thinking much bigger than just a hotel. I'm picturing a room for gambling, an inside swimming pool, an after-hours club, suites and my office overlooking the south end of the building."

Yandy sat down her plate. "What do you mean, your hotel?"

"C'mon, baby. You know what I mean. It's all our hotel but I'll be running it." He placed his hand on her shoulder and slid it down her slip. "Anything I do on the side will involve you too." He planted a kiss on her naked shoulder and her body quivered under his touch. "You're my woman."

"Mm," Yandy murmured softly. "I am your woman, and you bet not ever . . . ever . . . turn your back on me." She rested her head on his chest.

"Let's keep that extra money thing between us, okay?"

"Whatever you say. I'm with you."

Morgen sat behind his desk with papers and books scattered every-where while he talked on the phone, holding a burning cigar between his chubby little fingers. His righthand man, Frankie, sat in a chair reading a business magazine. Frankie dropped the magazine and went for the .357 Magnums under his arms when the door flew open but relaxed after he saw it was Yandy with Randy in tow.

"Aye, Yandy," he said in a thick Italian accent. "Try knocking next time, eh?"

Yandy cut her eyes at him as she walked past, and he noticed the bag she was clutching. "This is not your office, Frankie." Frankie remained standing with his gaze on Randy. Randy returned his stare without blinking as he gripped the black bags in his hands, ready to swing on them if it came to that. Frankie would be the first person Randy ever knocked out with three and a half million dollars.

"Who's this?" Frankie asked without taking his eyes off Randy.

Morgen removed the phone from this ear and covered it with his shoulder. "Everything's cool, Frankie. Have a seat." Morgen started talking into the phone again. "Steve, let me call you back. I got busi-ness over here . . . Un huh . . . Yeah, okay. Fax it over this evening. Goodbye." He hung up and caught his breath. "Everything went as planned I hear. The police and insurance company have been eating at my ass all morning. They have a problem believing all my banks getting robbed is just a coincidence." Yandy took out the bonds and placed them on Morgen's desk as Randy sat the bags of money on the floor.

"That's everything," Yandy explained. "You have something for us?" Morgen picked up the stack of bonds and regarded it carefully then went into his desk drawer and took out a stack of documents.

"It's all there. The deeds, everything. Take 'em and have your lawyer go over everything before you sign. You guys did a good job. Maybe we can do more business in the future, huh?"

Randy gathered the papers. "Maybe." He started for the door and Yandy trailed him.

"Aye," Morgen called to her. "Where you going, babe? I need you to stick around for a moment. There's a few things we need to discuss." Yandy looked at Randy and nodded her approval before she kissed his cheek.

"Call me later." Randy nodded then shot Frankie one last glare before exiting the office. After Randy left, Morgen stood and walked around his desk to the window, motioning for Yandy to come to him and she did. Morgen pointed out the window.

"See that?" Yandy glanced down toward the street. Cars were coming and going, roadside construction was being done, and people walked around like little ants.

"What?" she asked confused.

"The sidewalk. It's a long way down, isn't it?" He stared at the side of her face.

"Yes."

Morgen clutched her jaw in his hand so she grabbed his forearm. "Don't fight me," he warned and she released her grip. "If I find out you're fucking that black, slick bastard sonofabitch . . ." He pointed at the street below. "You're gonna find out the distance between here and there and you're gonna know how long it takes to get there, only you're not gonna live to tell." He squeezed her face. "Understand?" Yandy turned beet red in the face. Her instincts told her to knee his short ass in the balls but she knew that she wouldn't make it out of the building alive if she did so she simply nodded her head. "Good," Morgen replied. As soon as he released his grip, she stormed to the door. "Let me find out the black half of you is starting to override the white, you're fuckin' dead." She slammed the door closed. Frankie looked to Morgen with a puzzled look on his face. "What the fuck are you staring at?" Morgen asked harshly. "Get the hell outta my office." Frankie started to say something but instead acted like the flunky he was by doing what he was told.

While Yandy stayed behind with Morgen, Randy drove his rented Cadillac out to his new place of business. The first thing he would do was hire an architect to redesign the whole building. He wanted another floor added on top to hold six luxurious suites complete with Jacuzzis, stocked bars, Internet access, balconies and kitchenettes. Somehow, he had to obtain a permit from the gaming commission so he could open a casino on the bottom floor. There would be a real live gentlemen's room stocked with leather sofas, card and crap tables, slot machines, several flat screen TVs, a lounge area, and top of the line stereo equipment. His office would be built at the very top, surrounded by a bulletproof window that overlooked the entire banister area. Randy pulled in front of the hotel, got out, and inhaled the fresh air. For the first time in his forty-year-old life, he was really going to be s

ebody and it felt damn good. From that day forward, his life would consist of business meetings, expensive suits, coffee breaks, luncheons, flights, and power moves. And if it came down to it, cold-blooded murder.

"You got your chance, Randy," he said out loud. "Don't fuck it up."

The doctor blew his warm breath onto the cold stethoscope before placing it over Detective Madison's heart. He listened carefully while the detective took slow, deep breaths.

"Sounds good, Mr. Madison," the doctor informed him. "I think you're finally ready to leave this place." He pointed a wrinkled finger at Madison. "Don't forget to pick up the medicine I prescribed. We have to get that blood pressure of yours down."

Madison's wife helped him into his suit jacket. "He will, doc," she assured him. "Don't you worry." Madison grunted as he rose from the bed. Luckily, he was wearing his vest when he took the slugs the woman shot through his car window following the bank robbery. He growled in agony as he took his first step. "Careful, honey. You've been lying in a hospital bed for two days. You have to take it easy."

"Take it easy, my ass," Madison howled. "I can't wait to catch the scumbags that killed Blackberry." He patted his sides searching for his gun holster out of habit. "Where's my gun? Who's got my gun?"

"Baby, calm down," Shelby, his wife said softly. "It's in the trunk of the car with the rest of your things." In the car, Madison strapped on his holster then reloaded his gun while Shelby shook her head at him. For the last ten years, her super-cop husband had become obsessed with his job. She cursed the day he became head of the Robbery and Homicide Division. He turned her rearview mirror facing him to get a look at his reflection. His eyes were red and baggy, signs of old ag, and a beard was starting to sprout on his usually clean-shaven face.

Madison picked up Shelby's cell phone and started dialing numbers. "Yes, hello?" Madison said into the phone. "Get me Detective Law, please." He glanced at Shelby who was staring out of the window with a scowl on her face. He started to speak but Law came on the line. "Law, get me everything you can on every group of bank robbers that has a woman, starting from 1995. Then pull their files and the files of their known accomplices. Have 'em on my desk by eight o'clock tomorrow morning. Thank you."

Shelby sighed as soon as he ended the call. "There goes my quality time. It seems like the only time I get to see you is when you're sleeping or wounded."

Madison shook his head. "You know I got a job to do, Shelby. And part of it is to protect the citizens of this city. Look what happened. Two outstanding young cops lost their lives while trying to cash their checks."

"I'm sorry about that and I feel for their families, but sometimes officers die in the line of duty. That's their job."

Madison slapped the dashboard. "Not under my command, it isn't!" he yelled. After taking a few deep breaths, his voice lowered. "The fuckers who did this are gonna pay."

"Our justice system will—"

"Those bastards will never live to be brought to justice." He peered out his window. "Not if I can help it."

"Frankie, would you hurry the fuck up!" Morgen shouted impatiently. He and Yandy were standing in his office's garage clutching bags of money while they impatiently waited on Frankie to bring the limo around.

"Calm down, baby," Yandy said.

"What ya mean, calm down? We're standing out here holding over five million dollars and he's bullshitting." The tires squealed as Frankie bolted the stretch limo around the corner. He came to an abrupt halt directly in front of Yandy and Morgen. Morgen snatched open the back door, let Yandy in, and got in behind her. About a block away from Morgen's loft, the limo began violently jerking. Frankie pulled over to the side of the street just as the engine died, and Morgen instantly became nervous. He let down the privacy window. "Frankie, what the fuck is going on?" he asked in a worried tone.

"I don't know, boss." Frankie turned the key with no luck so he opened his door. "Let me look under the hood."

"Hurry the fuck up, would ya?" Morgen's body moved about in anxious gestures. "Brand new fuckin' car breaks down. What kinda shit is that?" Yandy put her hand on his shoulder.

"Calm down, baby. Everything will be okay." Suddenly, the back door opened, and Morgen looked up to see a bleeding Frankie being held by a masked man. A second masked man appeared out of nowhere. He reached in with his pistol drawn and grabbed one of the bags that Morgen was holding.

"What're you doing?" Morgen held on tight. "These are important business papers." Without any hesitation, the man hit Morgen upside his head with the gun. Morgen finally released the bag as he fell over on Yandy's lap. The man handed the bags to a third man who waited outside the limo. "You're not gonna get away with this, you fuckin'—" The man stared at Morgen as if he was contemplating killing him.

"Shhh!" Yandy murmured. "Don't do nothin' to make them kill us." She held his head in her lap. Finally, the masked man began to retreat. He stood, pointed a gloved finger in the shape of a gun at Morgen, then pretended to shoot him. Morgen blinked and by the time his eyes reopened the man was gone. Seconds later, he heard tires squealing. Frankie collected himself then wildly opened fire at the fleeing Impala.

# 6

Spud, Chuck, and Randy sat around the table in wife beaters, smoking cigars and laughing as Spud joked about how scared old Morgen looked while he was being robbed for five million. Chuck was dismissed after he was handed a small stack of cash and was told that the rest would be put into the hotel fund. After his departure, Randy handed Spud a much larger stack.

"You know he knows it was us," Randy said.

Spud shrugged. "Fuck 'em. What do we care? If he makes a fuss about it, we'll bury his fat ass under a bridge. Makes me no difference."

Randy patted him on the shoulder. "Chill out, ole buddy. I want to keep him alive for my own personal reasons. I heard he has mob ties. If I can get in close with him, then he may be able to help me get funded for what I'm trying to do."

Spud studied him carefully. "You mean we."

"Hm? Oh, yea, that's right. . . We."

"Good. So what's our next move?"

Randy cleared his throat. "Next we find someone to take the blame for what happened tonight then get rid of 'em. That way we'll earn old Morgen's unconditional trust." Randy stubbed out his cigar and stood. "Make sure you pay Frankie. Tell 'em he did a good job." Randy slipped on his shirt. "Oh, yeah. Before I forget, we need to find somebody to replace Alvin."

"You got somebody in mind?"

Randy nodded. "Name's Polo from out of Chi-town. I did four years with him in Leavenworth." He scribbled his name and number on a piece of paper then handed it to Spud. "Call him tomorrow and tell 'em to get down here. We got work for 'em." Yandy stormed into the restaurant headed straight for Randy. They stared at each other briefly before she drew her arm back and slapped him across his face. With the quick reflexes of a buck, he slapped her back. She swung again but he caught it and twisted her arm behind her back.

"Ow. Ouch!" she cried as he bent her over a table.

"Bitch, what the fuck is wrong with you?" he asked in a harsh tone. "'Cause if it's what I think you mad about, you'd better choose sides, fast."

"You fuckin' bastard! You could've warned me, Randy."

"We had to make it look good." Randy released his grip as Yandy snatched away from him.

Breathing rapidly, she pushed her hair out her face. "They scared me half to death. What do you need his money for anyway? Huh?"

"Yandy, we talked about this. You know what I'm trying to do. And to do it, I'll steal from my goddamn grandma. Don't act like you don't know me and my ways."

"You're right, I do know you. That's how I figured out who did it."

Morgen walked into the restaurant followed by Frankie and another lean-faced goon. He regarded Yandy with contempt then snapped his fingers at her. "Over here, now!" Yandy did as she was told, and Frankie grabbed her by the arm. Suddenly, Morgen bolted toward Randy and swung at him. Randy sidestepped the blow then pushed Morgen onto one of the tables, causing an ashtray and salt and pepper shakers to fall to the floor. Frankie hesitated but the other goon drew down on Randy. Just as quickly, Spud opened his thumper. No one saw Terry, who was over by the grill, grab his 12 gauge. Morgen wiped blood from his lip as he stood to his feet, and Yandy ran to his aid.

"Get away from me!" Morgen barked. "I followed your black ass over here."

"They're friends of mine, Morgen," Yandy explained.

"Don't give me that friend crap. You're fucking this nigger!"

"Call me another nigger, you ugly ass cracker, and we gon' tear this place up," Randy sneered. "Now what's going on?"

Morgen pointed his finger at Randy. "You fuckin' nig—y'all robbed me!"

Randy looked at Spud then back at Morgen. "Who robbed you? Point him out."

"Don't get smart with me. You know goddamn well what I'm talking about."

Randy took a seat. "You're right, I do. Yandy just told us everything. I'm sure that . . ." Randy paused and nodded toward the goon who still had the gun pointed at him. Morgen looked back and slowly gestured for him to put down the gun. After he did, Spud holstered his. Randy continued, "Like I was saying, I'm sure I can put my ear to the street and find out what happened. Maybe even get some of the money back."

"Why not all of it?"

Randy threw his hands up. "You're asking the wrong man. If these guys are black, they're sure to be spending your money as we speak." He lit a cigarette. "But if I do . . . If I do, you have to invest it into my hotel. Either that or you can find your own goddamn money." Morgen chewed his bottom lip while glaring upside Randy's shiny dome. He wanted the man in front of him dead but then he would never see his money again. All that money. He couldn't see himself just shrugging it off and taking that big of a loss. His hands were tied. For the time being, he had to do things someone else's way. Randy's way. His head bobbed up and down in thought.

"Alright, Randy. You've got a deal." Morgen put on a false smile and offered his hand, but Randy just stared at it.

"Smiles and handshakes don't fool me, Mr. Morgen. I know you'd love to shoot me right now."

Morgen snickered. "Many men have also wished death upon me, Randy. But just like you, I'm still here."

Randy finally accepted his hand. "Tell me, how do I go about obtaining a gambling license?"

Morgen smirked as if the man standing in front of him was joking. After he saw that he was not, he cleared his throat and began to speak. "What for? You're a felon."

"Assume the hotel and license will be under my mother's name. I'll secretly run it under another title. I want to open a casino inside the basement of the hotel. I plan on hosting fights, entertainers' after parties, and things like that. That's the only way I can see the hotel making a comeback. Otherwise, my friends and I are out of three million."

Morgen rubbed his sagging chin. "Sounds like a great idea. I want in. I can help get the funds to build this thing but I'll be expecting a big return."

"No deal," Randy stated firmly.

"No deal? The only way you'll ever be able to obtain a gambling permit is if I'm in on it. Who in the hell do you think you are? You'll never get it done without me. A lot of palms have to be greased. State politicians and people of that nature. Talk money out of investment bankers and make deals with Union pension fund officials. People you didn't even know existed, ones that carry big names and titles that you've never even heard of." Randy had never thought of it that way. Yes, he was getting in way over his head and would definitely need Morgen's pull to get him started. He looked to Yandy who nodded.

"Okay, Morgen. You do whatever it is you gotta do, and I'll guarantee your money back plus a large kickback for your trouble."

"I thought you'd see it my way. My people will be in touch." Morgen walked over to the door and turned around. "Don't forget to find my money." He snapped his finger at his two goons then disappeared out the door. Yandy joined them.

After they were all gone, Randy turned to Spud and said, "Sic Polo on whoever you decide to take the rap for the robbery. Then leak to Morgen that Frankie was in on it. That way, we'll tie up any loose ends."

"Sure thing."

Madison and Detective Law sat inside an enclosed room watching the film of the bank robbery. They were near tears after they saw two of their fellow officers get shot. The tape showed unclear images of the gunmen's faces, courtesy of Morgen. When Madison saw the outfit of the woman who shot him, he ordered the tape stopped.

"Zoom in on her shoes," said Madison. "You see that? We found the heel of that shoe inside the sewer."

Detective Law said, "Now we know exactly how they escaped." Madison stared at the screen with determination in his eyes.

"Does anyone besides me wonder how they discovered that escape route?"

Detective Law knew his boss well. "What're you thinking?"

"I think it was an inside job. Either that or these assholes had blueprints of the city. Did we find anything on crews that have female accomplices?"

"Yes sir," Law said. "Two of them. One is a group of street punks, but they're small time and way too unorganized to pull off something like this. And the other is run by this man." He opened a file and placed a picture in front of Madison. "His real name is Jesse Merrit, goes by the street moniker 'Spud'. Our snitches say it's because he's a short sharp dresser."

"Un huh. What else? Give me something we can use."

"He has a five-man crew that consists of one female. We haven't been able to get a name on her yet. They started out robbing and extorting drug dealers, and I heard Spud's name mentioned in that jewelry heist a while back. Never had enough evidence to get an indictment."

Madison smacked his gum. "Tell me more."

Detective Law continued reading the file. "The crew members are Alvin, who coincidently has been reported missing by his family, Big Boi, and Chuck. Like I said, we haven't got a name for the girl."

"Alvin?" Madison repeated. "Where do I know that name from?"

"His sister, Alvina, stole that baby from Truman Medical Center nine years ago."

"Oh yeah, the babynapper." Madison finally stopped smacking his gum. "Okay. I want a full surveillance team on these clowns around the clock. I wanna know how busy they have been and their next move. And I want the name of the mysterious female on my desk some time this week." He peered at the screen one last time. "We're gonna catch these scumbags."

Spud picked up Polo from the airport with Chuck in the backseat reading a newspaper. To Spud's surprise, Polo looked like a grimy, cold-blooded killer. It was an unusual look for a guy that Randy would hang out with. Randy usually rolled with men who appeared trustworthy on the surface but were sneaky as foxes.

"So, Polo," Spud began. "Tell me about yourself." Polo was black as shoe rubber with a long, slender face, a bald head, and eyeballs as red as hot coals. Jailhouse tattoos covered his entire upper body.

"I'm a cold-blooded muthafuckin' killa," Polo boasted in a scratchy voice. "I'll knock a nigga's head off. I just did twenty years in the penitentiary, stabbing and bustin' niggas' asses an' shit. I'm tellin' you, man, I just don't give a fuck." He made funny gestures and motions with his hands as he spoke.

"A killa, huh?" Spud asked.

"Hell yeah. Like I said, I just done fifteen years in the muhfuckin' penitentiary."

"I thought you said twenty years?" Chuck cut in. Polo looked at Chuck as if seeing him for the first time.

"Man, look, I done did so much time I really don't know how long I've been locked up. I do know this, give me a gun and a target, and I'ma nail his ass." He hit the dashboard with his fist. "Believe that."

Morgen sat on his ass behind his desk, hollering at Frankie about all the shit that had been going on. First the hotel then the robbery. Since Yandy wasn't around for him to vent, he threw the coals at Frankie.

"And I'm telling you, Frankie," Morgen spat. "If—" He was interrupted when the phone rang. "Hello? . . . Un huh . . . Are you sure? . . . You're positive? . . . I see. Thanks, Big Boi. I'll get right on it." He slammed down the phone, and rubbed his eyes. "Frankie, we have a problem." Morgen stated as he pushed a button under his desk, and Frankie sensed something was wrong. He stood with concern on his face.

"What's wrong, boss?" Seconds later four guys dressed in suits walked into the office.

"It seems," Morgen said, "Randy found the guys who stole my money."

"That's great. Isn't it, boss?" Frankie said.

"Huh? Oh, yeah, right, it sure is." Morgen looked away. "Look, uh, Frankie, I want you to make a run with the guys for me. I gotta little problem I need handled." Frankie turned and looked at the men standing behind him. They all wore blank expressions.

"Boss, you sure?"

"Yes, I'm sure. It'll just be a short ride. It'll be over in no time." Frankie stared at Morgen for a long moment. He wasn't a fool; he'd been around long enough to know what Morgen meant by it'll be over in no time. Randy gave him up. Now he had to pay the ultimate price for dealing with niggers.

Two of the goons placed hands on each of Frankie's shoulders. "Let's go." Frankie turned on wobbly legs and left the room with the goons in tow. Morgen hated to punish his longtime friend but it had to be done.

"Get off me! Get off meeeee!" Frankie's cries could be heard on the other side of the door.

## 7

It took over a year and $88.6 million dollars to reconstruct the hotel and add on the casino. In order to do so, Morgen had to bribe certain state politicians as well as make donations to churches and surrounding businesses. Plus, he had to obtain special permits and licenses. Things Randy couldn't do. Several investors chipped in to help manifest Randy's dream into reality.

Morgen had convinced them Randy being black could generate a young crowd by providing the right entertainment and various events, even make the hotel a popular tourist attraction where millions would come from around the world to sleep and gamble. Morgen believed in Randy, and the investors believed in Morgen. He had made them so much money in the past they couldn't refuse him. If they had, Morgen would have brought in his extortion team to muscle them until they were broke so there wasn't much of a choice.

The hotel and casino was beautiful. It was built with three hundred rooms, twenty suites, conference rooms, several restaurants, a children's playroom, a small arena, an after-hours club, and the casino was in the basement; secured by thirty guards, closed doors, and cameras everywhere. The casino area was called The Den and had all the comforts of a lounge. It was equipped with leather sofas, glass tables, designer lamps, and laptops with an open network. The walls were red brick and the floors were wooden to add the cozy feeling of home while the palm tree gave the room an exotic flavor. A sixty-inch flat screen accommodated every wall in The Den. They purchased the gas station that was across the street and knocked it down to build parking garages.

Randy's office was built at the very top but The Den was his favorite room. All he had left to do was find a group of fine females that could keep the ballers gambling until they were broke, some money-hungry groupies without a conscience or a soft spot for suckers. Straight thoroughbreds. To find them, he placed ads in the papers, ran a commercial on TV, and interviewed strippers but hadn't found the right group until the day he was standing in the hotel's parking lot, watching his "Reserved for Owner" sign being posted.

Loud rap music came blaring through the air. Randy faced left and saw a classic, drop-top '69 Camaro whip into the parking lot. It was painted bright red with tan Gucci seating and held up by gold twenty-two-inch Daytons. The beautiful car got his attention but what captivated him was the beautiful young woman gripping the wooden steering wheel in the driver's seat. She got out wearing black and white pinstriped slacks, high heels, and a white blazer. The diamond-studded choker around her neck almost blinded Randy from a distance. Her long and curly jet-black locks hung to her shoulders. She had pencil thin eyebrows with full pink lips and an exquisite nose, like that of a poodle. The young woman gazed in Randy's direction and squinted her eyes. The sun must have been too bright for her because she put on a pair of oversized shades. Randy scurried over to her in his tailor-made suit, Gucci glasses, and gators.

"Hello," he said cheerfully. "I'm Randy Harris, the owner of the hotel."

She shook his hand. "Jenny." Her tone was firm, yet very seductive but she gave him a sneaky vibe. He believed that she could slip the diamond ring off his finger without him knowing it.

"How can I help you?"

Jenny removed her shades. "I heard you were looking for a group of bitches to work your player's den."

Randy almost smiled at her bluntness. "Yes, I am."

"I command a group of young, fine, scheming hoes. Some of the best around, myself included, who will work any man that enters The Den. No matter the size of their bankroll, if they leave with fat pockets, it's because they've filled them with the complimentary peanuts from the bar." Randy smiled. Jenny smirked.

Without conducting an interview, he found himself saying, "You're hired."

"I promise we won't let you down, Mr. Harris." Jenny put her shades back on then got into her car and made the loud pipes came to life when she turned the key.

Randy put his hand on her door as she attempted to close it. "How about dinner?" he asked.

Jenny pursed her full pink lips. "How old are you?"

"Forty-one," he replied with a hint of embarrassment, though being locked up for fifteen years preserved his youth and had him looking a crisp thirty-two.

"I'm only twenty-two. You're old enough to be my daddy. Sorry." She giggled as she backed up her car then sped out of the parking lot.

When opening night came around, everything was set to go. The entire staff was in place, from the manager to the housekeepers. Snoop Dogg was in town headlining a concert and was having an after party at After 7, the hotel's after-hours club. Jenny and her crew were lounging in The Den and the girls were as fine as Jenny promised.

There was RiRi, a five foot seven Dominican chick with smooth slender legs, a round ass, and a handful of breasts. She had a small round nose and long sandy brown hair. Freaky Freeda, a little Korean beauty, stood all of five foot three but she was stacked. She came equipped with plump breasts, a sharp nose, and brunette hair that fell to the small of her back. A tattoo of a yellow dragon covered her right foot and ankle. Last but not least was Sasha. She was a redbone leggy chick who was almost six foot with short, crinkly hair and inno-cent schoolgirl looks. They all wore bright colored lipstick but different eye shadow and skimpy, exotic clothing covered their well-shaped bodies. Jenny wore a glittery thong with stilettos, her diamond-studded choker, and a fur draped around her naked shoul-ders. The only thing that shielded her huge, round false boobs were glittery stars that covered her nipples.

Randy stood on the staircase above The Den observing them as they sat next to different men on the sofas, chatting and sipping champagne. He observed their false smiles and gay laughs while they sipped with one hand and caressed pockets with the other.

"Look at 'em, Spud," Randy said with a smile. "A den full of thieves. All rested and made up for one purpose . . . to help me get rich. Isn't it beautiful?"

Spud smiled. "I have to admit. You done it, baby. That's why we handed it over to you."

"Goddamn right it is," Randy boasted with that hungry gleam in his eye. "Waitress! Get us a couple glasses of champagne. I wanna make a toast." He faced Spud then gave him that same devilish smile and handshake that even he wouldn't trust.

While sorting through mail inside his office the next day, Randy ran across a letter addressed to him with no return address. He carefully examined the envelope before opening it. Spud, who was lounging on the sofa adjacent Randy's desk drinking cognac, saw the suspicious look on his face.

"Everything alright?" Spud asked.

Randy looked up at him. "Yeah." He opened the letter and read it.

*A fool and his money will soon part.*

Randy put the letter inside his desk drawer. *What the hell is that supposed to mean?* he wondered. He remembered how brutal he used to treat both men and women when he was young. There were so many victims he could hardly name them all.

*Knock! Knock!*

His secretary entered the room. "Miss Jenny's fast tail is here to see you."

"Send her in, ma." Jenny appeared in the doorway looking fine as fur.

"Hey," Spud said with a smile. He was short enough to look her eye to eye.

"Hi, Spud," she replied. "Is the boss—Oh, there he is." Spud observed her rear through savage orbs as she swayed over to Randy's desk. He winked at Randy then left the two alone. "One of the rappers from last night is staying in suite 313. He's planning on staying the whole weekend, so I'll be clinging to him for the next forty-eight hours. Just so you know."

"How much did he lose last night?" He let his eyes wander down to her crotch where it looked like the shape of a perfect letter V. A tingling feeling jolted through his loins as Jenny took a seat across from him with her legs agape.

"I'd say . . . close to thirty grand, give or take." She spread her legs, giving him a clear view of her pantyless crotch. Randy sat up in his chair.

"Boy, you really know how to set it out, don't you?"

"And you're referring to . . ." He nodded toward her opened legs and she smiled. "That's not for your pleasure, Mr. Harris. It's for mine." Randy was confused. "See how big your eyes became when you saw it? Sweat started rolling down your bald head." She leaned forward. "You call that a kind of power 'pussy control.' It gets me off."

He shifted in his seat as he felt his dick stiffen. "Let me be blunt."

"Please do." Jenny kept good eye contact.

"Am I ever gonna . . . you know . . . be able to hit that? I mean, I am the boss here. Isn't that how it's supposed to happen? The pretty girls set it out for the boss, hoping to climb the corporate ladder?"

"In some situations," she admitted. Jenny removed her blazer, revealing a pink lace bra. She stood and walked around Randy's desk to where he sat. After she turned his chair to face her, she realized he was in his boxers and his dick was in fact hard. He kept a rack of slacks in his office closet but never lounged in them.

"My pants are in the closet," he answered her question before she could ask it. Jenny straddled him, pressing her round breasts against his nose. He took slow, deep breaths as he caught her Burberry perfume.

"You see that, Mr. Harris? Look at how you're sweating. I could do anything I want to do to you right now." Randy kissed her chest, and she felt his dick jerk, poking her butt cheeks. "See, you're the boss, but I can take control any . . ." she paused and licked his nose, "time I want." She rose and walked back to her chair, leaving him dumbfounded. While she put her jacket back on, Yandy walked into the office with her eyes glued to the real estate brochure in her hand.

"Baby, I saw some bad houses out in—" She froze when she saw Jenny buttoning her blazer. "What's going on?"

Jenny smirked at her then gazed at Randy. "Nothing at all." As soon as she opened the door to exit, Yandy pushed it closed. Yandy leaned over, putting her face close to Jenny's and noticed her poodle-like features.

"If the little pooch wants some more milk, she needs to find another bottle to suck on." Jenny inhaled Yandy's scent while she peeked down her blouse.

"You'd better watch your back. It could be breast milk these lips crave. Good day." Jenny opened the door and left. Even though they hadn't done anything, Randy still had a guilty look on his face. He came out of the closet with his slacks in hand.

"You were saying, baby?" He was hoping to avoid the inevitable.

"What were you two doing?" Yandy asked hotly. Randy sensed her jealously and decided to toy with her.

"Nothing that you and old Morgen haven't done." He put on his diamond R cufflinks as Yandy's mouth fell open.

"Now you wanna lay it all out on the table? That's not fair and you know it. I am too old to be competing with some firm-breasted, twenty-two-year-old child, Randy."

He slipped on his suit coat. "Hush up, old girl. I was just teasing you." He walked up on her and kissed her cheek. "I love you."

Yandy pulled away from him. "I love you too, but I am not about to play a game of chess with Jenny." Randy admired the beauty Yandy still possessed to be nearing forty. She was equally as beautiful as Jenny, only Jenny had that wonderful thing called youth on her side. While Yandy's breasts would begin to sag and she'd experience menopause in the next five years or so, Jenny would just be blossoming and able to bare the fruit of Randy's seed.

"Man, you are fine." Randy reached out for her. "C'mere." With little resistance, Yandy allowed herself to be pulled. Randy nudged her earlobe with his nose.

"That tickles," Yandy murmured. "Stop. Stop, baby!"

"No matter how old you get, you'll always be new to me." Those words took her breath away.

"Aww, boo, give me a kiss." They hugged and kissed passionately for about two minutes until Yandy felt moisture in her underwear and pulled away. "Stop, we have to meet the lady about your house."

He desperately started humping her leg. "She'll wait if she wants the money bad enough." He tried to kiss her again.

"Noooo, bae, I'm starting to leak in these little ass panties."

"Let me suck 'em dry."

"No, silly," Yandy giggled. "I want you to follow me out that door so we can go." She made for the door and Randy gruntingly followed behind her. When the elevator opened, they saw the rapper and Jenny going at it. She was kissing his neck while he lifted her skirt then propped her foot on the rail. The rapper turned around and saw Randy. He had on shades, a sweat suit and a long platinum chain dangling from his neck.

"You better get on if you comin', dawg. There's plenty of room for you and your lady friend too." Yandy and Randy stepped on and faced front while Jenny was behind them purring like a helpless kitten. She knew that she was getting Randy aroused. His was jealous too but he couldn't get mad. She was doing what she was being paid to do; take care of the guests and keep them spending.

"Mmm," Jenny purred. "Gambling makes me horny."

"Does it?" the rapper said in a rehearsed cool voice. "Well let's go down to The Den and get about ten thousand worth of chips to try our luck."

Jenny smirked. "Win or lose baby, I'm still gonna . . ." she whispered the rest into his ear. They both giggled when she finished. "It's all good, baby."

Yandy leaned in close to Randy and whispered, "Want me to suck your dick while we're on the elevator so you can look cool too?"

Randy looked at her and frowned. "C'mon, now. You're a lady so act like one."

"I was only gonna do it for you." As Randy stepped off the elevator onto the first floor, he wished like hell he would have at least one shot at getting Jenny. No matter what the cost.

## 8

R andy and Spud trailed behind Morgen while he entertained some big men from the governor's office that personally came to get a look at the new hotel and casino. Just by looking at Randy you couldn't see that he was nervous but he was dropping fingernails everywhere he walked. Spud snuck away for a brief moment then returned with a drink for him. They toured the restaurants, then the club, and stopped and chatted by the pool. The two big shots were really checking out the bathing suits.

After about an hour of bullshitting, Morgen led them down to The Den. It was crowded with all kinds of different income from drug dealers and ball players to businessmen and whoever else could afford to gamble big. Randy took control and led them over to the lounge where they ordered drinks and enjoyed the scenery. RiRi sat at the bar as planned, sipping on a Sex on the Beach while Sasha stood over her with their legs intertwined, caressing her shoulder. Every card dealer in the club was female and they were made to wear boy shorts and stilettos to look appealing to the customers. Halter tops were also standard dress so they couldn't conceal any stolen chips.

The governor's assistant, Karl Peters, stared at RiRi and Sasha. He saw RiRi's strap slide off her smooth shoulder, as Sasha dabbed a pinch of salt on it, took a drink of tequila then licked it off before they tongue-kissed one another.

"Sweet Jesus!" Karl bellowed. "Would you look at that!" The five gentlemen shot flirtatious looks across the room the bar as they continued to watch the exchange. Sasha had her hand on RiRi's crotch, rubbing it while Sasha sucked liquor from her finger. Jake, who was also from the governor's office, cracked a smile.

"Nice place you got here, Mr. Harris. Love your choice of female company," Jake complimented.

Randy finished sipping his drink before he responded. "Thank you. Say, how would you gentlemen like to get to know those two lovely ladies?"

Karl waved Randy off. "Stop it. What do we have that they want?"

"I'm 'bout to find out." Randy sat his drink down on the small square table. The four guys watched him strut over to the bar and make conversation with the two women who found him humorous. After about a minute, the girls climbed off their stools and followed Randy back over to the lounge with their arms locked in his.

"Oh my God! Here they come," Karl exclaimed. He and Jake straightened their ties and ran their fingers through their hair. Jake's was badly receding so he didn't have much to do.

"Gentlemen, these lovely ladies here are RiRi and Sasha. I told them y'all work for the governor, and they wanted to meet you personally."

"May we sit with you guys?" RiRi asked.

"Sure, sure." Karl was excited. He scooted over on the sofa so the girls could relax between him and Jake. Randy gestured for Spud and Morgen to stand up.

"Ladies," Randy spoke, "why don't y'all show these two a good time."

Sasha touched Jake's crotch. "Ooh, don't worry. We will be good," they giggled.

"Remember, gentlemen, you have to pay to play. Nothing in this world is free." The girls were getting acquainted with the two dorks when Freaky Freeda appeared out of nowhere. She had on a two-piece swimsuit, fishnet stockings, and knee-high boots.

"Somebody order a five-some?" she asked.

Karl loosened his tie. "The more the merrier."

Freeda hopped on his lap. "You're gonna have to show some green if you wanna freak Freeda." Both dorks raced for their wallets.

Randy, Morgen, and Spud walked away to survey the floor.

"Ooh! We won, baby!" Jenny shouted. She was at the crap table throwing the dice for her rapper friend. When Randy stopped to watch her, he saw her cut her eyes at him. She winked then continued with what she was doing.

Morgen grabbed his balls. "Boy, would I like to stick my prick inside that kisser."

"You're not the only one," Spud replied. Randy observed her for a second longer before walking away, but Yandy watched the whole episode on camera from the security room. She could tell by the look in Randy's eyes he had an ache for Jenny, one that could only be healed by hours of passionate sex. Then hopefully, after his cravings were satisfied, he would come back to her. If not, Yandy was in a world of trouble. She had killed for cash but what would she do for love? That was the question she had to ask herself. Truthfully, she didn't know. Probably because she had never been in love with anything but money.

Over the next six months, the business prospered enormously. Every week there was an event going on at the hotel. Whether a title bout or an after-party, something was going on. Randy had rigged the machines so a certain gambler would win a two hundred and fifty-thousand-dollar jackpot that made the news and gamblers started pouring in from everywhere. He leased four brand new Cadillacs for the company executives and purchased a half million dollar home.

The crew was becoming salty because Randy had started spending majority of his free time with Morgen and a bunch of other powerful white men. He joined clubs they couldn't join, hung out in places they weren't wanted, and even avoided them whenever they tried to meet with him. Spud was still his main guy but he was more like a right-hand man than a business partner. Whatever Randy needed done, Spud did without question. That was how it had been since they were kids.

Yandy was still his girl and wherever he went, she went. She was a lovely woman who worked the room at all their parties. She even accompanied him to the governor's mansion and to conventions in Vegas. She regretted not being able to move in with him because of her promise to Morgen but now she was ready to break it and marry the man she loved. Unknown to her, Randy was content with the way things were. That way, he could spend more time chasing Jenny. He had tried everything. Gifts, free suites, and sweet talk but hadn't struck gold yet. Randy felt defeated and was beginning to believe what she had told him in the first place. He was too old for her.

Smokey Robinson sang, "Baby let's cruise, awayyy from herrrre," through the factory speakers of Randy's new Cadillac XLR as he rode with the top down. The sun beamed on his slick dome while he rounded Hillcrest Road on his way to work. The world was his, he thought, and the law couldn't touch him. He had gotten too big too fast and was in cahoots with all the right people. From lower level mafia men to state politicians, prosecutors, judges, teachers and athletes were now part of his guest list. They would do anything and spend any amount to keep partying in his den of whores. In fact, Jenny and Sasha had been proposed to by several top federal authority figures but they declined, claiming that they were hoes and not housewife material. Breaking bankrolls was not only their occupation, but their narcotic as well. It was what woke them up in the morning. They loved who they were, and Randy loved them, especially Jenny.

Randy himself had contemplated proposing to Jenny and he hadn't even had a drink with her, let alone sex. What was it that made him crave her so? Jenny played hard to get. No matter who it was or how much cash he banked, she always remained in control of herself and the situation. Loud rap music could be heard over the sounds of Smokey as tailpipes growled behind him. Randy glanced at his mirror and saw Jenny's Camaro rounding the bend at a fast pace. She had on her shades and was singing along to the song with her three road dawgs with her.

They looked like they were kicking it as their long hair blew with the wind. Jenny was a car length behind him when she crossed over the yellow no passing line in the northbound lane. About a block or so ahead, a small car drove straight toward her but Jenny pulled alongside Randy. He peered over at them like they were crazy. The passengers all sat up in their seats then flashed their titties at him. He fought for control of the wheel while trying to watch them and the road ahead. They continue to shake titties and blow kisses at him.

*Beep! Beep!*

Jenny waited until the car got within one hundred feet of her before she stepped on the gas and swerved in front of Randy.

"You bitches wanna play?" he said aloud. After the car passed, Randy crossed the no passing line and floored it. Jenny saw him passing on the left so she shifted gears and accelerated as well. They both gazed at each other while their cars approached max speed.

*Vroom!*

They were running neck and neck when a truck came driving over the hill. The driver saw the Cadillac and immediately began honking his horn. Randy hit the gas some, hoping to pass Jenny, but she kept accelerating.

"This bitch is crazy," Randy said to himself. As the truck neared, Randy thought fast. He didn't want to let up and let her win but he didn't see any other choice. Freeda and RiRi started doing the chicken. Randy thought about running them off the road, but her Dayton helicopter knock-offs might have taken out his tires. The truck continued to honk so Randy released the pedal and swerved back over to the right lane behind Jenny.

The girls clapped in triumph as they pulled into the hotel's parking lot. They were parked ten feet away but loud laughter was heard while they exited the car. He gazed at the four women with admiration. They were bad, witty, and classy all at the same time. And they were young. Randy watched Jenny smirk as she strutted towards him wearing army capris, stilettos and a tank top.

"I told you I was in control, boss," she said with unhidden sarcasm. When she tried to walk past, he seized her arm.

"When are you gonna learn a woman's place?" he asked.

"When I become one. Right now, I'm just a gangsta ass bitch who wants to have fun."

Randy smiled at her. "And what is your idea of fun? A cruise to Jamaica? Thousand dollar shopping sprees? What? You name it, I can make it happen."

"My idea of fun is having hard, butt-naked sex while thizzin' on X while plotting to steal a nigga's check." She smirked while looking him up and down. "You . . . all you wanna do is spend big bread with hopes of taking me to bed at the end of the night. Then when it's all said and done you'll only hit and run, all the way back to your lonely little wife."

"Poetic justice," Randy replied. "I do wanna hit it, you're right about that, but I also wanna get to know you." He released his hold.

"Do you know that I have the stamina of three women?"

"You're young."

"And you're old," Jenny retorted. "I'll tell you what. Be waiting in suite 326 after midnight. You'll get your chance to show me you still got it." She spun around and led her crew inside the hotel. Karl, from the governor's office, was sitting in the lobby waiting for Freeda.

He jumped from his seat when he saw the four of them walk in. "Hey, ladies," Karl shouted. "I've been calling you all week, Freeda. Where have you been?" Randy patted him on the shoulder as he walked past. "Mr. Harris, don't forget we're doing eighteen holes this weekend," Karl reminded him.

"I won't. I'ma practice shooting a few holes myself tonight."

"Good, good," Karl murmured then gave Freeda his undivided attention.

"You bring some money?" Freeda asked, and Karl reached for his wallet.

"Yeah, I—"

"Good, let's go upstairs."

Just before midnight Randy stood at the front desk inside the lobby, barking at the clerk about being rude to the guests. While he did that, Jenny walked past and slipped him a note. Randy pointed a long finger at Gina, the desk clerk.

"One more time, Gina. One more time and you won't have a job." He stormed off. He waited until he was on the elevator before he read the note.

Don't forget, suite 326 after midnight

When he stepped off the elevator to his office, he tossed the note in the trashcan. Inside, he found Spud and a white woman he knew as Faye fondling each other on the terrace.

"Spud," Randy called as he started taking off his clothes. Spud left the girl outside and rushed to his aide.

"Yeah?" He saw that Randy was getting undressed. "Whoa! We can't share this one, playa."

Randy sneered. "I don't want none of that stankin' ass white bitch. Here," he tossed him his key ring. "Keep an eye on my hotel. I got some business to tend to." Asshole naked, he walked to the shower.

Spud toyed with the keys while glaring at Randy's back. *His hotel?* Those words puzzled Spud.

# 9

R andy inserted his master key in the door and slipped into the suite. All the lights were out but Usher's "Trading Places" played from someplace in the room. He let his eyes adjust to the darkness before he took another step.

"Lay down on the bed," Jenny's voice said. "It's five steps forward and four to the right." Randy did exactly as he was told. As he sat at the edge, the lights came on but were dim. Out the shadows came Jenny holding onto a leash. Sasha, Freeda, and RiRi had chain-linked collars around their necks. They crawled on all fours in front of Jenny as if she was their master. "Like I said before, boss, I have the stamina of three women. Conquer this obstacle then maybe I'll give you a taste." Jenny unleashed them. "Sic 'em." They all stood up naked and crawled onto the bed. Randy couldn't believe his luck. Roughly, they began pulling off his clothes while Jenny only watched.

Sasha and RiRi playfully fought over Randy's dick with their lips. One would get a few licks then nudge the other to the side like two kittens fighting over a toy. They decided to split up with one taking the balls while the other sucked him off then they would switch. Freeda squatted over his face and growled loudly as he gripped her ass and munched on her clit. Jenny stood at the edge of the bed, watching with an expressionless face.

Freeda climbed off Randy's face and walked over to the table where she picked up a joint. She lit it but didn't inhale. Randy was lost in the zone when she crawled back onto the bed. She took a long drag then pressed her lips up against his, blowing the smoke into his lungs. Randy sat up coughing and gagging, so Sasha patted his back. Then she took a puff and blew the smoke into his mouth as well before RiRi followed suit. He took a deep breath as he lay back, experiencing the greatest head rush he had ever felt. It was so intriguing he couldn't figure out why he felt that way.

He felt lips, tongues, titties, and teeth gnawing at his body. When his eyes fluttered open, he saw Sasha bouncing up and down on his joint. Her eyes rolled back in her head as she humped herself into an orgasm. When she finished, Freeda straddled him backward then held on for the ride. RiRi lay between his legs and started sucking his balls while she restlessly awaited her turn. Suddenly, the glorious high he felt disappeared just as quickly as it came.

Randy sat up on his elbows. "More! More!" he hollered. "Give me more!" Sasha relit the joint, puffed on it, and blew it into his lungs while holding his nostrils closed. RiRi sucked on his balls, causing him to explode inside of Freeda. She climbed off thinking he was done, but Randy flipped RiRi over in the doggy style position and planted himself deep inside her velvety walls. Her back arched deeply as she felt the painful, yet pleasurable feeling shoot through her body.

"Harder!" she begged. "Uhh! Uhh!" He lost control of himself as he started pounding into her viciously, as if he was trying to inflict bodily harm. RiRi begged for him to kill it. She gripped the sheets while he clamped her small waist, forcing herself backward. Freeda smacked RiRi's ass, and Sasha slid under her and sucked her titties.

Yandy lay in bed unsatisfied after having a two-minute sexual encounter with Morgen. He was snoring on his side while she let thoughts of Randy and Jenny hover inside her head. Recently, all her nights were spent the same. Sleepless. She couldn't stand the idea of having to leave Randy at the hotel with Jenny. Yandy wasn't hating on the younger woman, she was just jealous. She peered at the clock on the wall and saw it was just after midnight. She smiled at the thought of arriving at Randy's office wearing nothing but a fur coat and heels. Yandy snatched up her robe and ran to the shower. She was excited because she had been wanting to do that ever since she saw it on TV years ago. After she tapped Morgen a few times to make sure he was asleep, she left the apartment.

When Yandy pulled outside at the valet, she made her face up in the mirror before exiting her car. She wore a chinchilla coat with no clothes or panties underneath and stilettos. She had smoked a joint on the way so she was feeling pretty good. Upon entering the hotel, she observed guests lingering about in the lobby. Loud music was blaring from the club around back while women ran around in bathing suits, headed towards the pool area. Yandy had the desk clerk call Randy's office to see if he was in but he wasn't. That disappointed her but she knew he was somewhere near because his Cadillac was parked outside.

She hopped on the elevator to The Den. As soon as the doors parted, she stepped into a whole new atmosphere. People were gambling, loudly laughing, and drinking. Some were even dancing. The cocktail waitresses were running around in skimpy little outfits taking orders and being hit on. Suited men were lounging on the sofas chatting perversely with women while sipping expensive champagne. Yandy guessed there were more females in the den than inside the club. All of them were chasing the almighty dollar. Yandy's jewelry glittered with the many lights as she swayed around the room, hunting for Randy. Every suited black man with a bald head wasn't him.

She was almost discouraged until she spotted Spud at the bar surrounded by four white women. They were all smiles while they were being entertained by the small man. Yandy walked up to him and tapped him on the shoulder. Spud automatically reached for his gun as he spun around. He was at ease after he saw Yandy standing there smiling.

"What the hell is wrong with you, Yandy?" Spud hollered. "You know you can't be sneaking up on me like that. Niggas want my head. I can't get caught slipping."

Though he was right, Yandy ignored him. "Have you seen Randy?"

Spud noticed how good and young she looked. Had they not been partners, he would have made a pass at her a long time ago. Somehow, Randy had slid in and up in her. "Yeah," Spud answered. "He's upstairs in his office."

Toward the end of the bar, a medium-sized Italian man with dark hair sat next to a tall, white man with a red mustache. The shorter of the two was Detective Madison and the tall one was his partner, Detective Law. They were eavesdropping on Spud's conversation while having a few beers. They watched carefully as Yandy marched away from Spud back to the elevator before Spud resumed his conversation with the beautiful women. Big Boi was over at the crap table, losing a shitload of money while Chuck was upstairs in a suite entertaining two underaged girls. Madison turned around on his stool and faced the crowd.

"Well, they've done it," Madison spat. "Finally made the big time. They've gotten away with enough capers to open a fuckin' casino in my goddamn town." He raised his beer mug. "Here's to Spud fuckin' Brim." He took a big gulp as Law glared at Big Boi. He was standing between two chicks screaming at the dice.

"Believe me, these guys won't stop here. I mean, there's too many fingers in this pot for them to turn much of a profit." He took sip. "Besides, stealing is in a nigger's blood. It's just a matter of time before they make their next move. You'll see."

Madison tossed some bills onto the bar. "I hope you're right." He surveyed the place one last time. "Let's go." Outside, Madison handed the valet his ticket. He lit a cigarette while he waited on his car. After glancing to his right, he saw Randy's Cadillac in the "Reserved for

Owner" spot. "Law?" Madison asked. "I thought you said this place is owned by several investors."

"It is, Residue Entertainment. Why?"

Madison pointed at the Cadillac XLR as he approached it. He took out a small notepad and wrote down the license plate number. "This sign here says reserved for owner, not owners." He flipped it closed then stuck it back inside his jacket pocket. "Something fishy is going on here, and we're gonna get to the bottom of it."

Yandy stepped off the elevator and saw Jenny scurrying across the hall into Randy's suite. *What is she doing coming out of Randy's office?* she thought. She was just about to grab the door handle when she heard laughter behind her. She saw Jenny, RiRi, Sasha, and Freeda exiting another suite. The group of women stopped when they saw her. They were half dressed, looking like they had just finished banging one another.

Jenny smirked. "Hey, Yandy. If you're looking for the boss," she nodded toward the room, "he's in there taking a shower." They walked away giggling to themselves, and Freeda purposely dropped her underwear on the floor.

"Excuse me," she smiled as she picked them up. Yandy saw steam coming from the shower when she entered the room. With anger in her eyes, she stepped into the doorway. Randy heard heels tapping against the marble floor and ignorantly mistook her for one of the girls.

"One of y'all get in with me. I think I can get him up one more time," he laughed. Yandy slid the door open, and Randy's smile disappeared when he saw her standing there naked. For a moment, he didn't know what to say or what to think. She stepped inside the shower and beads of hot water attacked her honey colored body. She stared at him seductively as she cupped his hands then placed them on her breasts.

"What's the matter?" she asked in a husky voice. "You can't get him back up for me? Hmm?" She reached down between his legs and clutched his limp organ. "That's funny. You were able to get it up when you thought I was one of those freaks." Yandy faced the opposite direction, held onto the wall, and arched her back. Reaching back, she spread one of her butt cheeks. "C'mon, Mr. Harris, don't you still find me attractive?" Randy said nothing. "I know what you want." Yandy dropped to her knees and attempted to kiss his dick.

"Yandy, stop!" he yelled as he pushed her back, causing her to hit her head against the tile wall. "What the fuck is wrong with you?" He shut off the water before he stepped out. He snatched a towel off the rack on his way to the other room and Yandy followed. Randy slipped on his robe then lit a cigarette.

"I'm not pretty to you anymore?" She stood in front of him. When he didn't respond, she snatched the cigarette from his mouth and threw it. "Answer me, damnit!"

"Bitch, you better calm down." He tried to step around her, but she stepped in his way. "Move, Yandy. You gon' fuck around and get the shit slapped out you."

Yandy placed her hands on her hips. "Here I am. Slap me, muthafucka! What, you're mad 'cause I caught you—"

*Wack!*

He slapped her onto the floor. "You're too tough for your own fuckin' good, bitch," he hollered as he glared down at her. "You ain't no damn man, you a bitch. And you better start learning how to stay in a bitch's place real quick." She held her hand up to her face while pretending to still be woozy. As soon as he came in reach, she kicked him in the balls. "Aaah!" he cried as he fell to his knees.

Yandy picked up her stiletto as she stood up. She shot daggers at him while she circled him. "You've got the wrong bitch, Randy." Yandy plucked him on top of the head with the heel of her shoe and his face fell toward the bed.

"You bitch," he murmured.

"Aw, yeah?" Yandy kicked him in the stomach. Then the back. Then the ass. When she finished, he lay curled up on the floor in pain. He tried to get to his feet but the punch to his nose sent him back down. "Lie there and think, bitch," Yandy spat. "'Cause you just lost the best thing that ever happened to your arrogant ass." Yandy put her shoes and coat back on then left the room. She bumped into Spud on her way out.

"You alright, Yandy?" Spud inquired.

Yandy peered back at the doorway then down at Spud. "No, I'm not alright. My feelings have been hurt." She strutted to the elevator.

Randy crawled to the doorway yelling, "Stop that bitch, Spud!" He tried to get up and run but tripped into Spud. Yandy waved at him teasingly as the elevator doors closed.

"Randy, grab a hold of yourself," Spud said. "Man, that's Yandy!"

"I know who the fuck it is." He snatched Spud's jacket open and reached for his gun.

"Naw, man, you tripping." Spud pushed him away. "Pull yourself together and tell me what happened."

Randy started toward his office. "Unlock this goddamn door." Spud fumbled with the keys until he found the right one. Randy barged in and ran straight for the balcony. He peered down in time to catch Yandy getting into her car. "I'ma have yo' ass dealt with, you fuckin' bitch!" he yelled as spit surrounded his lips. "Yo' ass won't live another night."

"Try it, you cocksucker!" Yandy yelled. "You's a bigheaded nigga but you wouldn't be shit if it weren't for us!" Spud tried to grab him, but he snatched away.

Randy leaned over the iron railing shouting, "I did this, bitch! I put all this together. I negotiated the deals. Me, me, me!" Yandy smirked while she gazed at him making a fool of himself. His robe blew open, exposing his naked body, and a small crowd began to gather down below.

"You hear that, Spud? He did everything by his goddamn self. We couldn't have had nothing to do with it." Shaking her head, Yandy got into her car and drove away.

Randy turned around and stormed toward the bathroom, bumping into Spud along the way. "I want that bitch hit, Spud. You hear me? Dead before the devil finds out what's going on." He slammed the bathroom door. Spud sighed while he gazed up at the star-filled night sky. Randy was getting out of control and Spud had no idea what to do to stop him.

## 10

D *ing, ding, ding, ding!*
"I won! I won! I just won ten thousand!" the lady exclaimed. She jumped for joy as the coins flowed out of the machine and into her bucket. Two guards rushed to her aid to offer her protection until she left the casino. Jenny scanned the entire room from the sofa while Freeda was at the bar watching as well. RiRi was on the dance floor but she was still aware of her surroundings. Sasha was at the craps table, rolling the dice for some hustler. Two armored-car guards walked in, one carrying two bags and the other holding on to a pistol. They walked through the room, almost unnoticeable, and into the count room on the far west side of The Den. Jenny could only catch a quick glimpse of the room before the door swung closed. No one was allowed inside the room except for the counters and armed guards. The guards spent exactly ten minutes inside the room, according to the time all four women kept, then they snuck back out the casino. All four women looked at one another and nodded.

Randy sat with his vest open on his large sofa, drinking champagne in front of his giant TV screen with his two Dobermans sat on either side of the couch. Robert De Niro was on TV in the movie *Casino* and Randy was taking notes. He had already watched it four times that week. The ears on both dogs stood erect as vicious growls escaped their mouths. Randy hurriedly picked up the remote and pulled the security monitors on the screen. He saw Spud's Cadillac Deville parked at the front gate so he pushed a button that opened it. Minutes later, Spud walked through the front door. He examined the spacious, luxurious living room of the house, the high angled ceilings, Italian furniture, and the cozy stone fireplace. One would have thought that Randy had lived that way all his life. That was, if they didn't know any better. Randy sat picking his teeth while he glared at the TV screen. Spud removed his suit jacket then took a seat in the chair next to the sofa.

"Spud, you take care of Yandy?" His eyes never left the TV.

Spud dropped his head. "Nope." Again, Randy picked at his teeth. "I haven't summed up—"

"Never mind," Randy interrupted. "I've got something else planned."

"I'm listening." Spud fired up a cigarette. Randy gestured toward an alligator-skinned briefcase that rested on the table in front of

Spud, so Spud opened it up. It was a photograph of a blond man in an expensive suit. "What's this?"

"Fredrick Bewig the Fourth. He's an associate of Morgen's. Said to keep a black notebook in a wall safe inside his home office."

"So?"

"So, I want it," Randy stated before he finished the rest of his drink. "Morgen wants it, and he's willing to pay a pretty penny for it."

Spud gazed at Randy with greedy eyes. "How much?"

Randy sighed, "A million dollars."

"Any help on this one?"

"Yeah, he'll be at the golf club until six o'clock Thursday evening. Drives a chauffeur-driven Lincoln."

"Who is he?"

"Some guy who owns a company Morgen wants to take over. The book contains his personal strategies and whatnot."

The phone rang and Spud got up to answer it. "Hello? . . . Just a moment." Spud handed the phone to Randy.

"Hello?"

"It's Morgen. Have you talked to him?" he sounded anxious.

"Just a minute." Randy peered at Spud curiously and Spud nodded. "It's all good, man."

"Thank you, brother," Morgen replied with satisfaction.

"You'll thank me enough after I get my money." Randy hung up and gave the phone back to Spud.

"You comin' along?" Spud asked as he returned the phone back to the charger.

"Nope. I'll be on the golf course with Fredrick. I'll call and inform you when he's departing." The dogs growled again and Randy switched to the security screens. Jenny's Camaro was at the gate. Randy's blood started pumping as he jumped up. "Make yourself scarce, Spud. I got company." He hit the button that opened the gate then disappeared into the other room. Jenny was getting out her car when Spud came out the house and gazed at her slim figure candidly. She smirked as she passed him, leaving behind her sweet fragrance for him to feast on. He couldn't help but peep the gold underwear she wore under her transparent skirt. Her stilettos tapped a beat against the concrete as she swayed up to the door. Spud tossed his cigarette down and got into his car. A black Volvo was parked across the street but it wasn't there when he first arrived so it sparked his attention. He stopped his car next to it and peered in the window but saw no one so he drove away thinking nothing of it.

After Spud pulled away, a woman's head popped up and she watched Randy give Jenny a hug in the doorway. He had changed over the years. His body appeared to be solid from the distance. The dread-locks he once wore were shaved, leaving an oval-shaped gleaming bald head. Yet, he still turned her on after all the years of drama he took her through. She had to admit that. When Jenny and Randy disappeared inside the huge house, the lady skipped across the street and dropped a note inside his mailbox then quickly returned to her car and pulled off.

"I got your note," Jenny said as she sat her purse on the table. Randy walked toward her with two champagne glasses and handed one to her.

"Obviously, you showed up." He shut the TV off. "Let's go out back." Jenny followed him through the luxurious home to the kitchen and out the back doors. There was a statue and a fountain surrounded by a stone patio, manicured shrubs, plants, and flowers decorating the entire yard. Across the way, Jenny could see a small guest house. Off to the right was a three-car garage and to the left was a polished gray stone platform that housed a Jacuzzi. Randy led her over to one of the benches where they both sat. For a while, they drank in silence until Jenny finally spoke up.

"So, why did you ask me to come here?" The look in her eyes intimidated Randy so he looked away.

"Because I passed your stamina test. Now it's time for you to put out."

"Put out?" Randy peered down at the huge princess cut diamond on her finger, pondering what to say next. Jenny smirked. "Age has made you insecure, you know that? I watched you and Yandy. She's very pretty but you handle her like she belongs to you. Like you're in control of y'all situation," she giggled as she slid closer to him. "But for some strange reason, when you're in the presence of a young . . . fine . . . tender like me, you humble up." She put her face close to his but when Randy leaned in for a kiss she backed away. "Did I say kiss me?"

"No, but—"

"But nothing. If you want to lay with me, you have to admit one thing." She grabbed his cheeks with her hand. "And that is . . ."

"You're in control," he said in a low whisper. Jenny stood while gazing down on him. Before he knew it, she let her skirt fall to the ground but her huge round implants demanded his attention. She placed her foot on the bench between his legs.

"Kiss my foot." He did. "Now, remove my shoe and suck my toes." Her facial expression had turned into that of a slave master but Randy did as he was told. He poured champagne on her knee and let it run down to her toes. He heard a soft moan escape her lips as he slowly brought her foot to his mouth and gently sucked each one of her little toes. Jenny let her head fall back with her eyes closed, enjoying the feeling. He tongue-fucked her toes so well her natural juices soaked her panties.

The cool night's breeze and the cold champagne on her legs gave her goosebumps. "I'm cold," she stated. He stood, scooped her up, and carried her inside to his bedroom. He walked up the two-step platform next to his bed then gently laid her down. Randy crawled on top of her and started sucking her breasts while Jenny caressed his bald head. For the moment, she seemed to be in total submission. She reached inside his pajamas and stroked his organ. Using his free hand, Randy pulled his pants down over his butt as Jenny was jerking him off. Carefully, he eased her panties down and over her feet then tossed them. A completely shaved, dripping wet pussy stared him in the face. He bent her leg to where her toes were damn near touching the headboard and her wet crevice glistened. He thought about tasting that young nectar first but he was too eager to get inside of her velvety walls.

Just as he was about to enter her, she screamed, "No! Stop!"

"Huh?" he asked confusingly.

"Get up! Get up!" The second he released her she jumped up, grabbed her panties, and left the room. Randy didn't know what to make of the situation as he stood and pulled up his pants. He was walking out the room when Jenny shot past him with her skirt and heels in her hand, flying out the front door.

"Jenny, wait!" he called after her. She got into her car and fired up the engine. Randy hit the button that opened the gate for fear she would drive through it. Besides, it was no use trying to force her into doing something she didn't want to do. For all he knew, she would end up shouting rape. He figured she would give herself to him when the time was right. The flag on his mailbox was standing so to take his mind off things he walked out the front gate, opened the box, and took out a letter but there was no writing on it. He glanced at his surroundings to see if anyone was there. Other than the cars driving up and down the busy street all seemed well.

Randy closed the box then jogged back inside before he plopped down on the sofa and opened the envelope. It was a letter and a stack of photographs. Each picture appeared to be a young lady's face but there were no clear shots of who she was. They were only close-ups of her swollen lips, a bruised eye, and a broken nose. She was reminding him of who she was and what he had done to her. Only problem was, Randy had beaten so many women in his past it was hard to pinpoint which woman this was. He sat the pictures down and unfolded the letter.

*Dear Randy,*

*As I remember, you used to possess a natural instinct that alerted you of danger. How come you can't sense it now?*

## 11

---

T he tour bus of comedic actor Dave Chappelle pulled into the parking lot of the hotel. He would be performing three shows for three nights and the after parties would be held at the hotel's club, After 7. Of course, Jenny and her girls were standing outside the bus to greet the star and his entourage. They all looked stunning and sexy in high heeled boots and skirts. Dave took one look at the selection of women, all from different ethnic backgrounds, and knew he had chosen the right spot.

"I'm fuckin' all four of y'all," he said to them after he stepped off the bus. Freeda and Sasha gave him a look of approval as they escorted him inside. Randy adjusted his tie and cuffs as he stood in the lobby waiting to greet the man with Spud to the right of him. Security from the hotel and Dave's entourage were everywhere.

"Mr. Chapel," Randy said with a smile as they shook hands. "I see you've met my ladies. They'll be more than happy to assist you with all your personal needs and desires. Thank you for choosing my hotel for your stay."

Dave nodded. "Make sure me and my crew get a whole floor to ourselves 'cause we come to kick it and fuck some of y'all freaks so we gon' be very, very noisy."

"Your manager already took care of your reservations in advance." He faced Freeda. "Would you show them up to their floor, please?"

"Certainly, Mr. Harris," Freeda say gaily. "Right this way." The group walked toward the elevators and Jenny took up the rear, holding the hand of Dave's tour manager. She winked at Randy as they strolled past, and Randy felt a jolt go through his scrotum. He wanted her so bad he would do almost anything to get it, even marry her if he had to.

Spud nudged Randy. "What happened between you two last night? I know that young, hot ass is sweet."

"Nothing happened," he said regretfully. "That bitch played me like I was in high school. I got the little bitch butt-naked on my bed with her legs pinned back. As soon as my dick came within an inch of her, she jumped up, grabbed her clothes, and left."

"No fuckin' way."

"I couldn't believe that shit. I'm damn near forty-two years old."

Spud laughed at him. "Man, let's go get a drink. We got some shit to discuss."

"Do me a favor and keep that between me and you. That shit gets out, all these bitches will be trying to play me for a damned fool."

"Fuck that, man!" a drunk white man yelled. He was inside the casino, stumbling away from the Black Jack table. "I just lost my whole income tax refund," he burped. The Absolut Vodka was working on him. His friend was walking beside him trying to hold him up. "Four fuckin' thousand dollars I lost tonight." He pushed his friend away from him. "Get off me, you dumb fuck. I can't go home like this." He rested his elbows on the bar. "My wife's gonna fuckin' kill me."

The bartender gazed at him from across the bar. "Hey, baby," she said in an attempt to calm him down. "Why don't you just go home and get it over with?" She patted his shoulder in a comforting manner but Beavis jerked away from her.

"Don't try to comfort me, ma'am. I'm not a goddamn, baby."

She pushed her hair out of her face. "Go home, Beavis, okay?"

"It ain't okay!" Beavis yelled. He was big, about six foot three weighing two-hundred and seventy pounds. "I want my fuckin' money back." Randy and Spud walked into The Den while Beavis was going off. They heard the commotion going on to their right. The big drunk man stumbled over to the card table, and Joyce, the card dealer, looked terrified. "Give me . . . my fuckin' money back, bitch," Beavis demanded. He picked up the drink of the man sitting next to him and downed it. His face and nose wrinkled as the hot, bitter-tasting liquid traveled to his stomach. "What the fuck is that, piss?" Beavis threw the empty glass at Joyce, as Joyce called for security.

The little, brittle old man whose drink Beavis took frowned. He was an ex-boxer from the seventies. It had been a heck of a long time since he used his once powerful overhand right hook but he had been wanting to use it again for almost thirty years and finally had the chance. Tommy "The Machine Gun" saw security coming. He knew if his jab wasn't effective they were going to step in and intervene anyway so he went for it. He drew back with all the strength he could muster and hit Beavis in the nose but the punch had no effect. Beavis stood glaring at the man as if nothing happened just as security rushed him.

Tommy stepped out their way while holding his sore fist. Without even thinking, Beavis hit a guard in the face and kicked another. Then two more guards attacked him. Beavis' big country ass started slinging people everywhere. He accidentally hit himself upside the head.

"C'mon, you black motherfuckers!" he challenged. The guards attacked him simultaneously, seizing his arms and feet as they lifted him in the air.

"Take this piece of shit out back and flush it," Randy commanded. "Spud, you go with 'em." The guards rammed Beavis' head against the exit door to open it as Spud followed them out. While everybody was concentrating on the scene Beavis was making, his friend was busy swiping chips from the tables. Randy tried to get the crowd back in order. "Everything's okay, people. Please, continue gambling." He left The Den and headed out back just as the guards slammed Beavis on the ground. So many of them started kicking him he couldn't count them if he tried. Spud pulled out his gun then grabbed him by the hair.

"Aaah!" Beavis hollered.

"I don't ever wanna see your fat ass near this place again, you hear me?"

"Yes."

"Huh?"

"Yeess." Spud raised the gun then brought it down on Beavis' forehead.

*Wack! Wack!*

Beavis sprawled out on the pavement. "Ever again, you piece of shit." Spud put his gun away as he followed the guards back inside.

Just as Spud finished with Beavis, Randy was called upstairs to the camera room to review the tape. "Where is he now? Did he get out?" Randy inquired.

"No, he's staying in room 210. He's in there now." Randy got on the radio and called Spud.

"Yeah?" Spud answered.

"We got a thief in room 210. Why don't you go up there and check it out?"

"Will do." Spud alerted two backup security guards and led them upstairs. He stood back while one of them knocked on the door.

"This is hotel security. Open up!" Anderson sat on the edge of the bed counting the chips. When he heard knocking at the door, he damn near panicked. He took off his shirt and raked the chips into it.

*Knock! Knock!*

Anderson quickly glanced around the room for a hiding place and his eyes settled on the bathroom. He dashed inside and snatched the lid off the back of the toilet.

*Boom!*

The guards kicked the door open and rushed in to look around the room for him. Spud spotted Anderson's hairy back through a crack in the bathroom door.

"Get that son of a bitch," he commanded. The two guards rushed him before he could close the lid. They clutched his arms then dragged him into the other room.

"Wait a goddamn minute!" Anderson yelled. "What's going on?" Spud casually removed his jacket and laid it over the back of the room's chair as security threw Anderson to the floor.

"I'ma show you how we deal with thieves. Pick 'em up." The guards held him in an upright position while Spud went to work on him.

Randy walked into his office, placed his jacket on the rack, and sat behind his desk. Out his drawer, he removed some important papers.

"Mr. Harris?" his night secretary said through the phone.

"Yes?" he asked after hitting the intercom.

"A Detective Madison is on the phone for you." *This late at night? It can't be about nothing good* he thought.

"Tell him to call me tomorrow. And remember, I'm not the boss, I work in the entertainment department."

"Yes, sir." Randy sat back in his chair trying to imagine what the detective wanted with him. He froze when he saw a silhouette out the corner of his eye. Quickly, he reached for the gun that was clamped under his desk.

"Don't bother," Yandy said as she stepped out the shadows with tears in her eyes. He relaxed after he saw who it was. Her hands fidgeted when she approached his desk as she noticed how powerful and distinguished he looked in his suit. "I've been thinking." She placed her hands on his desk, unable to give him eye contact. "I'm sorry."

"You're sorry?" Randy snickered. "Is that all you have to say to me?"

"I shouldn't have hit you." She finally looked at him. "Randy, I've been in love with you for years."

"Step around here." He was stone-faced. Yandy slowly walked around his desk and kneeled before him. Randy slipped his foot out of his shoes. "Take my sock off and kiss my foot." Yandy saw the serious look in his eyes. Gently, she removed his sock then placed a soft kiss on his foot. "Now stand up and remove your clothes." Yandy stood and shucked her dress to the floor with ease. She was braless but bent over and pulled off her stockings and panties. While she was doing so, he thought about what Jenny told him. She said he controlled Yandy, and she, Jenny, had control over him. Yandy undid his pants and pulled them down to his thighs. After stroking his dick until it was hard, she straddled him.

Jenny stepped off the elevator carrying a bottle of champagne and two glasses, but Yandy's loud cries of pleasure could be heard in the hallway. Jenny stopped for a second to listen.

"Ah! Oooh!"

Suddenly, Jenny backed away. It seemed like it took forever for the elevator to return. In the meantime, she stood there with her ears tormented by Yandy's moans of pleasure. She rode the elevator to the main lobby, clocked out, and walked to her car. The tires on her car squealed as she bolted into the street. Jenny popped the bottle of champagne then turned it up to her lips. She pulled to a stop at the intersection of Seventh Street as a police patrol car was traveling north on Blue Ridge. Jenny hit the bottle one more time then tossed it out on the street, causing pieces of broken glass to scatter on the road. The cop driving the patrol car slowed to a stop after he saw the bottle flying out of the Camaro.

The top on Jenny's car retracted, she put on her driving shades, revved the engine, and hit the gas. Her rear spun sideways as she made a sharp right turn. At first, it looked as if she might lose it but the car straightened and proceeded. The police activated his sirens and got in pursuit. Jenny watched the speedometer accelerate at a quick pace before she looked in the mirror and saw two more cars had joined the chase. She sped past cars and through red lights. When she shifted gears, the Camaro's ass dropped and fire spit out of the exhaust as her head bobbed to the imaginary music inside her head.

A patrol car parked at the Longview intersection laid down tire spikes but it wouldn't stop her. When she neared the intersection, she swerved into the opposite lane then made a sharp left. She was rolling now with the wind blowing through her hair. The thrill of being chased did something to her body that she was unable to explain. After she made a right on Food Lane, which was a straightaway, the policemen watched her tail lights disappear before their eyes. *That should do it* Jenny told herself. Just before she hit Main Street she brought the car to a screeching halt. She took the time to light a cigarette while she waited on them to catch up. Soon, she was surrounded by patrol cars. Policemen leaped from their cars with guns pointed at her. She spit out the cigarette while she lifted her hands toward the sky.

"Step out of the car. Now!" one of them ordered.

Yandy held her palms firmly against Randy's desk while he pumped her from behind.

"Haaa! Haaa! Uhh!" Yandy was left gasping for air when he pulled out and collapsed in his chair with dick still standing. His tank top was soaked with sweat. Yandy put on his button-up shirt and went to the bathroom. Seconds later the shower came on. After a while, she returned with his robe in her hand.

"C'mon, let me clean you up," she said. He stood and walked over to her, and she gazed up at him. When he peered into her beautiful eyes, he saw love and passion. Yes, she really loved him. To her, he was more than just a fling, he was her world. Randy kissed her.

"Tell me you love me."

"I love you, old man."

His hands traveled down to her butt. "I think I'm ready to go another round."

"Ooh, you must've have popped a Viagra tonight."

"I think you gon' need one."

"No, I don't. I'm not even forty yet," she reminded him. He popped her on the ass as she took off for the shower. The phone rang and he prayed it wasn't that detective calling him again. "Hello?"

"It's me ... Jenny." Randy peered at the bathroom door.

"What you want?"

"I'm in jail. Can you come get me?" He didn't respond quick enough. "I can just spend the night at your house if you don't mind. I need to get out of these filthy jail smelling clothes."

*Damn* he thought. "Uhh, ye-yeah. I'll be there in a minute." Randy slowly placed the phone back on the base.

"Baby," Yandy called. "Hurry up before I get cold." He ignored her and sat in his chair to think. What was he going to tell Yandy? If he didn't come up with a good lie in a hurry, they were going to break up just as quick as they'd made up. He had to ask himself if Jenny was worth losing her. Randy put his pants and shoes back on. He stopped at the bathroom door, contemplating going in and doing it the right way. *But why?* he thought. He didn't have to explain himself to no one. The shower door slid open and Yandy stuck her soapy face out.

"Randy? Randy?" She rinsed the soap off her body then stepped out. Yandy grabbed a towel and wrapped it around her. "Randy?" She glanced around the empty office baffled. The phone rang and Yandy pulled her wet hair into a ponytail as she made her way to answer it. "Hello, manager's office."

"Has Randy left yet?" Jenny asked, well aware of what she was doing.

Yandy placed her hand on her hip. "Who is this?"

"This is Jenny. He was supposed to be on his way to pick me up." Yandy was afraid to speak knowing Jenny would hear her voice crack so to save face she just hung up.

## 12

J enny was already sitting on the steps at the police station
when Randy drove up. When he saw her, he wondered how
she got out without him. Had it all been a hoax to get him to
come? He honked the horn at her, and Jenny picked up the
brown paper bag that held her things and got into the car.

"How did you get out?" Randy inquired.

"My bondsman sprung me. He's a friend of mine." She fished her
cigarettes out her sack.

"Then why did you call me?"

Jenny sneered. She didn't like the rise in his tone. "I called your
office and some woman told me you were busy. That's why I had to
get out myself."

*Yandy. Oh my God* Randy thought as he pulled out the lot. He
wouldn't be able to lie his way out of this one if he wanted to. He dug
into his jacket pocket and removed his cigarettes. Jenny sat back and
relaxed on the leather seat, enjoying the cool nighttime breeze. She
looked over at Randy to examine him. He saw her but kept his eyes
forward. He was angry with her for making him ditch Yandy for no
reason. Jenny would definitely have to come off some pussy in order
to make that up. Randy stopped at the local liquor store to pick up a

bottle of Amsterdam Vodka, orange juice, and two cups of ice then hit the highway headed for Lookout Point by Washington Street.

"Where are we going?" Jenny asked.

Randy smiled. "Someplace romantic."

Jenny returned his smile with a warm smirk. "That's cool with me." Lookout Point was almost empty except for a van parked in the middle of the circular parking area. It was occupied by two teenagers who were sharing a bottle of Blue Dot Cîroc, trying to work up the nerves to screw. When they saw the other car pull up, they jumped in the back. Randy backed in a spot about three spaces from them and popped the trunk. Jenny grabbed the liquor while he put in a Jodeci CD to set the mood. It was chilly so he took a couple of blankets out the trunk.

"What are we listening to?" Jenny joked.

"Jodeci." He seemed baffled. "Don't tell me you're too young to appreciate good R&B music?"

"I'm a music fanatic, I was just joking with you. You're too self-conscious about your age."

"Shit, you would be too if you spent majority of your young life behind bars." They found a nice spot on the grass that overlooked the downtown area. He helped her wrap the blanket around her then poured two warm cups of vodka to help heat up their blood. Jenny tasted hers while he wrapped himself.

"Whew! Needs some juice."

"I thought you were the baddest bitch?" He opened the bottle of juice and poured some into her cup.

"I am but I like to watch what I put inside my body." She tasted the mixed drink. "That's better. So tell me about Randy Harris." She gazed at him, studying his handsome face.

"Like what?"

Jenny shrugged. "Tell me how you ended up in prison. What did you go through while you were in there? Things of that nature."

Randy took a big gulp then sat his cup down. "It's a long story. I shot and killed my baby's mama's brother in front of her. She called the police and had me locked up." He stared out into space. "You know, when they found me guilty, I looked back at her and could've sworn . . . I saw a smile on her face."

"What about your baby?"

Randy finished the drink then poured another before he answered. "Never saw her again. She's grown now and probably in school or pregnant. I did some fucked up shit to her."

"Wanna talk about it?" Her voice was comforting.

"Her brother stole some money from me. He was young, probably about seventeen, I don't know. I threatened to kill my girl and kid if he didn't return my money. When he did, I shot him in cold blood, right in front of her and my child."

"Would you have done it?" She watched him intently.

Randy pondered the question. "Back then . . . I might have just to show him I meant business." He took another gulp. "Back then, I just didn't give a fuck. I loved the sound of my gun going off. Someone could wave at me, and I would instantly become angry then lash out at them. My little girl saw enough in six years of living with me to be a coldhearted something. Plus, it's in her blood."

"Sounds to me like you miss her."

Randy sighed. "I did while I was locked up. It can get lonely on the inside. In jail, you miss things as little as walking barefoot on carpet. Isn't that ironic?" Jenny stood and got inside of the blanket with him then wrapped her long legs and arms around him. He relaxed under her tender touch.

"I probably smell like that funky jail, don't I?" she giggled.

"Baby, it wouldn't matter to me if you smelled like an outhouse right now. I just wanna be with you. I wanna marry you. I wanna . . . wake up to you every morning."

"There's a lot that comes along with me."

Randy shook his head slowly. "It don't matter. The road I'm traveling on now is headed north, and I can't lose. Everything you need and want will be handed to you." He pressed his lips against hers. At first she was hesitant to open her mouth, but due to the intimate moment they shared, she eventually gave in. For the next hour or so, they sat quietly, holding each other and keeping each other warm. They drank out of the bottle of vodka until it was gone. Then they got up and danced to the smooth grooves of Jodeci's "Forever My Lady". When it got too cold, they sat and talked some more. Finally, sometime around four o'clock in the morning, the liquor started to catch up with Randy. His speech turned into a slur, so Jenny helped him into the passenger seat of his car. Across the lot sat a Volvo facing their direction with the lights out. The woman that occupied it went unnoticed as she watched Randy stand in the seat.

"The world is mine. All mine!" he yelled. Jenny urged him to sit before they both ended up in jail this time around. She pulled him down and locked him in the seatbelt.

"Let's see what this baby can do," Jenny said. The brand-new engine purred when she started it. Randy held on while she cut corners until she got on the highway. She then went ninety miles per hour. Cautiously, she weaved in and out of traffic lanes, just barely avoiding collisions. She glanced over at Randy to see how he was handling her reckless driving, and he looked like he was about to puke at any given moment. She smirked as usual but didn't slow down any. The tires squealed when Jenny turned onto Randy's street. She hit the button in the eyeglass visor that opened the gate. After she parked, she helped him inside. He was sluggish and heavy.

"Lights," Randy barked upon entering the house and all the lights came on. Jenny helped him to the bedroom and his heavy body fell onto the bed, shaking up his stomach. "OHH!" he moaned. Reaching up, he pulled her on top of him. Jenny giggled as she straddled him and began kissing his neck and face. His body relaxed while she removed his clothing. He was so drunk he was near unconscious. Jenny gazed into his eyes hypnotically. "What's wrong?" Randy asked curiously. Jenny got up then went to the living room. She returned a minute later with a joint inside her hand. She climbed up on the bed next to him, fired it up, then passed it to him. "Is this the same shit as last time?" She nodded and Randy accepted it. He took a long puff, holding the smoke inside his lungs as long as he could.

She sat back and watched him through mischievous eyes. "Hit it again, baby," she urged, and he did as he was told. The smoke hit his lungs so hard it made him gag. He lay back on the pillow with his eyes closed, unable to move his lips. She removed the joint from between his fingers, laughing silently.

Law snapped pictures of Randy's car and home from the passenger seat of Madison's car parked across the street and he got a couple shots of Jenny helping Randy into the house. They had been watching his every move since earlier that day. So far, the investigation came up blank. They had learned nothing other than he was a killer and an ex-con who had done time in prison.

"Get a few shots of the dogs too," Madison said. "They can go down with him." Law got two shots of the dogs while they were resting next to Randy's Cadillac.

"What do you think of that hot piece of hot ass he's got with him?" Law asked. "I'll bet she cost a mint, huh?"

"Yeah, I'll bet." Madison sucked his teeth. "Criminals. They have all the fun, don't they? The guy gets out of prison just a couple of years ago and is secretly heading a multi-million-dollar business. A gambling business at that." He shook his head as Law stared at the house.

"I don't know. I mean . . . maybe we're jumping the gun here.

Maybe the man is head of the entertainment department like he says he is."

Madison peered over at him through suspicious eyes. "You switch sides or something?" The stare that Madison gave him made Law shift in his seat.

"No, Man. I'm just saying, everything ain't always as bad as it seems."

"Of course, it is. That's why we're here. Don't you forget that." Law sat the camera down and opened his door. "Where are you going?" Madison inquired.

"I need to make a call."

"What, you don't want me to hear what you're saying?"

"It's private," Law said with a smile. "Give me a minute, okay?"

Madison peered at Randy's window. "I'm gonna get you, you slick fuck."

# 13

R andy stood in a golfer's stance while gripping his putter and measured for the shot. Fredrick Bewig and his personal caddy stood five feet away, looking.

"You might wanna tighten your butt cheeks just a little bit, Harris," Fredrick joked, hoping he would miss the putt.

"Thousand bucks says I sink it," Randy said.

"You're on." Just as Randy was about to hit the ball, Fredrick yelled, "Fore!" Randy hit the ball too hard, causing it to veer too far to the left. He glared over at Fredrick who had his gloved hand over his mouth, snickering.

"What kinda shit you on, man?" Randy asked hotly.

"You have to holler 'fore' before you hit the ball, Randy," he chuckled. "I thought you knew that." Randy pulled out a wad of bills and counted out ten hundred-dollar bills. He held the money up then dropped it on the ground by his feet. Fredrick didn't take offense to it. Instead, he snapped his fingers and ordered his caddy to get it. The man pulled his slacks up at the knees, bent over, and picked up the money. A huge grin was glued to Fredrick's face when he accepted the cash.

"A fool and his money will soon part." It didn't take long for

Randy to remember where he heard that saying before. It was written on that mysterious letter he received.

Gripping his club tight, Randy asked, "You say that a lot?"

Fredrick took a break from counting his winnings to look up. "Say what?"

"That thing about a fool and his money."

"Yeah, it's something my old man used to tell me when I was a kid. Why?"

"Not important." Randy relaxed. He laughed inside thinking how true that statement was. Only Fredrick didn't know that he was speaking to himself.

Fredrick sunk his putt. "Ha, ha! I win again."

"Give me a little time, Fred." They loaded themselves onto Fredrick's golf cart and rode back to the club. He ordered his caddy to take care of his things then glanced at his Rolex watch. "Ooh, it's getting late, Harris. I have to fly to Hong Kong early tomorrow."

"A pleasure playing with you. Have your people call my people so we can do this again." They shook hands and the arrogant businessman strutted out the door, dialing on his cell phone as he made his way to his limo parked out front. Randy peered out the front door at the Buick Century parked on the north end of the lot. When Fredrick's limo drove away, the Buick followed. To kill some time, Randy took a shower then sat inside the steam room for a while.

Polo was behind the wheel of the Buick Century while Spud rode in the back seat behind him and Big Boi rode shotgun. Spud had yet to start trusting Polo. Every time they were around one another, Spud kept a close eye on him. He talked too much and told too many lies. Spud would feel more relaxed if the man would just shut the fuck up sometimes. He had to smoke a cigarette to calm his nerves.

"Like I said, we oughta run in there and cut that cracka's throat wide open," Polo suggested. "In the joint, I woulda cut his asshole open to hide all my knives and dope in it. Make that bitch carry it around with him, like a . . . a fuckin' human stash spot." Big Boi and Spud looked at each other before they burst out laughing.

"Where did you get this guy, Spud?" Big Boi asked.

Spud had to regain his composure before he could answer. "Man, I don't know. Randy found this crazy ass fool in the joint, I guess."

Polo's eyes shifted from Big Boi to Spud's reflection in the mirror. "What the fuck's so funny?"

"You," Spud said. "Yo' crazy ass belong in the nuthouse some damn where."

Big Boi pointed out the window. "He's pulling into the gas station."

Spud got on his cell phone. "Do it here."

"Do what?" Yandy asked. She was about half a block behind them.

"I don't know. Improvise."

She let out a long, frustrated sigh. "Okay." While the limo driver filled up, Fredrick walked inside the store and talked away on his cell phone on the way to the cooler. The bell on the door jingled when Yandy walked through it. Her eyes searched the area for Fredrick and she found him bent over, reaching inside the cooler. Just as he found the drink he was searching for and stood, he felt something, or someone, bump into him. When he turned around with a frown on his face, the first thing he saw was a long, smooth set of legs. He thought he smelled her fragrance but the cold air coming from inside the cooler smothered it. His eyes traveled up her legs to her thighs, over the hills of her breasts then rested on her smiling face.

"Excuse me," she said in her most cheerful voice. "How clumsy of me. I didn't see your cute little butt sticking out of there."

Fredrick flipped his phone closed, hanging up on whoever he was talking to. "If you think my butt is cute," he said, "you oughta see the rest of me."

Yandy pretended to be offended. "I don't think so. Excuse me." When she attempted to walk away, he grabbed her arm.

"I'm sorry," he apologized as he released his grip. "I just didn't want you to walk away angry at me." He offered his hand. "Fredrick Bewig."

"Not the same Fredrick Bewig who owns the Bewig toy company?"

He put on a cocky smirk. "That would be me." He gestured toward the window at the limo waiting outside. "I'm shocked you know of me. How so?"

After running her fingers through her hair, she said, "I used to work for you."

"Used to?"

"Yes. Unfortunately, women who work for your company seem to have a hard time climbing the corporate ladder, no matter how qualified they are."

His handsome face softened. "I'm sorry to hear that, Mrs . . ."

"Miss," she corrected. "Just call me Margo." They shook hands but she pulled away when he began to caress hers.

"Well, Margo," he said, "you do know in this day and age there are various ways for a woman to get into an executive position? It doesn't always boil down to what she knows or how many degrees she has. Sometimes it's as simple as . . . a one-night stand that keeps them from escalating." He shot her a knowing look. "Need I say more?" Yandy pretended to be contemplating an answer. She nervously looked to the left then to the right.

Finally, her mouth opened. "Your place or mine?"

He smiled. "Mine's nearby. You can follow my limo there."

The limo driver looked constipated as he held the door open for his boss to get into the back. Fredrick was going to say something but quickly disregarded it when images of Yandy lying naked across the bed flooded his brain. "To my estate, please." The driver nodded without saying a word before he closed the door. Yandy followed the limo inside the gated driveway. As Fredrick hopped out talking on his cell phone, his two dogs rushed him. "Down! Down!" he shouted. "Jesus! You're gonna ruin my pants . . . Yeah, Morgen, I'm here." He motioned for Yandy to follow him inside as the driver took his position to the right of Fredrick. Yandy walked past them into the house. While Morgen was yapping in his ear, Fredrick visualized Yandy's big lips wrapped around his massive white cock. Fredrick covered the phone and whispered to the driver, "After I'm finished with her, come up with an excuse for me to kick her out."

"Like what?"

He shrugged. "Doesn't matter. I gotta get some sleep before my flight tomorrow."

"Sure, boss." Fredrick disappeared inside. Polo was hiding in the front seat of the limo the entire ride. When he saw Fredrick go inside, he stepped out the car. The driver was scared half to death.

"Good job," Polo said. "I didn't wanna have to step out that car firing."

"What now?"

"Open the gates so my friends can get through." The driver did as he was told. Meanwhile, Fredrick stood behind his bar with his back to the security monitors as he mixed two drinks, but Yandy saw the Buick driving through the gates.

"Why don't we cut to the chase and go straight to your bedroom?" Yandy said, distracting him. He immediately stopped what he was doing.

"What, no appetizer?"

Yandy shook her head. "I'm ready for the main course." Fredrick felt his nature rising in his pants. He set the mixed drinks down, walked around the bar, and gazed at Yandy sitting on the barstool before he stuck his tongue inside her mouth.

"Mm," he grunted. "You're such a whore, you know that?"

"Yes." Yandy tugged at his pants. *He likes to talk dirty* she thought. "And you're such a stud, baby. Let me see it."

"Whip it out, you slut." Yandy undid his pants then reached in, pulling out one of the biggest dicks she had ever seen. He dangled in front of her and the sight of it shot spasms through her crotch, almost making her forget the plot. Her ambitiousness and female lust made her want to test her skills by seeing if she could swallow it all but she remembered she was not a whore and this was only an act.

Spud, Polo, and Big Boi followed the driver through the house. "Where is he?" Spud inquired. The driver started to cry so Polo slapped him across the face. "Where is he?" Spud asked again and he nodded toward the stairs. They all took out masks and pulled them over their faces.

"Take care of him, Polo," Spud commanded then he looked at Big Boi. "C'mon." The driver peered at Polo with terror in his eyes.

"What's gonna happen to me?" His lips and hands were trembling.

"Shit, what you think? Yo' ass is 'bout to die," Polo said coldly, staring at him through his bug eyes. "Hell is in your future." Polo stabbed the driver to death then caught up with his crew at the top of the circular staircase. They heard the music, but couldn't figure out which room it was coming from. It seemed to be echoing throughout the entire mansion.

Fredrick and Yandy had shucked their clothes and jumped into his jet stream hot tub as jazz played through the speakers on the wall. His head rested on the cushioned edge while Yandy straddled him, kissing his hairy chest. Fredrick reached for his glass but the water on his fingers caused it to slip out his hands and the broken glass scattered across the floor.

"Damnit!" he cursed.

Spud turned to the left after he heard the glass break. "This way." They stood outside the bathroom door as Spud put his ear to it but only heard the saxophone playing. He placed his gloved hand around the knob and turned.

"I'll get it, baby," Yandy said, referring to the broken glass.

"No, no! You just relax. I'll get it." Fredrick stepped out of the tub naked, and Spud could see the pink side of his ass and balls while he was bent over to clean the shards of glass. Fredrick got the feeling someone other than Yandy was watching him. He peered back between his legs and saw a masked Spud glaring at him. "Shit!" Fredrick tried to run to the other door as he heard Yandy screaming for help. "Gomez!" he yelled. When he reached for the door, he slipped and fell. Spud grabbed him under his left arm and Big Boi grabbed him under his right. Polo came from behind landing vicious jabs to his kidneys. Fredrick yelled and screamed but it was no use. By the time Polo was done beating him, the man was barely conscious. Yandy grabbed her clothes and made a run for it.

"Stop her!" Spud ordered.

"I got that bitch," Polo said as he took off behind her.

Spud looked down at the bloody man lying on the floor beneath his feet. "Now that you know how serious this is, I trust you'll tell us where that safe is."

Polo came running back into the bathroom out of breath. "I couldn't catch the bitch," he panted.

"Well we gotta move fast." They dragged Fredrick all the way to his bedroom.

"Please!" he cried.

Polo yelled, "Shut the fuck up!" Spud and Big Boi slammed him on the thick carpeted floor in front of his bed. Polo kneeled, glaring at him with his bug eyes wide open. "You scared as a muthafucka right now, ain't you, honky? Yeah, you scared." Polo slapped him across the face. "Look at me when I talk to you." Fredrick's chest was heaving rapidly. He looked up at Polo's masked face with terror in his eyes. He wanted to cower away but didn't want to get struck again.

"My wallet is on the dresser," Fredrick offered. "Take it and leave. Please!"

Polo smacked him again. "You know goddamn well we didn't come for no fucking wallet. Get up!" He snatched Fredrick up then pushed him toward the door. "Take us to the money."

Fredrick spit out a clot of blood. "I keep my money in a bank. There's not much here." Spud peered at Big Boi then nodded his head, and Big Boi left the room to search the house. Polo walked over to the closet and found a crocodile-skinned belt. He wrapped it around his hand on his way back over to Fredrick.

With a sneer on his face, Polo said to Fredrick, "I'm about to whoop you like you a useless dog."

"Owwww!" Fredrick screamed after he received the first lash across his back. Spud fired up a cigarette and admired the artwork on the walls while Polo punished the man. Big Boi ran down the stairs, searching until he found Fredrick's office. It was furnished like it belonged to a college professor as a massive collection of books covered the entire south side wall. First he scanned the painting along the walls but found nothing. Then he looked over to the book-shelf, and there in the middle, he found what he was searching for. He took out a book titled *Mr. Promiscuous* by Ace Gucciano and a few more books. Next he stuck his hand inside the empty space and felt the metal exterior of the safe's door then the knob. After he jumped to his feet, he pulled out his Nextel to hit Spud.

"I found it," Big Boi informed. "I'm downstairs, second door on your right."

"Okay." Polo stopped beating Fredrick. "You lying muthafucka, you." He reached down and snatched him up. "Get up! Get yo' ass downstairs and open that . . ." he hit him again, "goddamn safe." Whips and bruises covered Fredrick's back and ass. His body was in pain as he limped into the hallway then down the steps. It seemed like it took him forever to get to the bottom. To him, it was no longer about the money, he just wanted to get Polo away from him. He hoped the girl had called the police and they would arrive before the intruders escaped. Stalling was the furthest thing from his mind because there was no telling what Polo would do next.

Fredrick led them inside his office with snot and tears covering his once handsome face. The powerful businessman looked more like a wounded boxer than a corporate executive. Big Boi stood in front of the bookshelf with books scattered around his feet and waved them over. Polo put his hand on the back of Fredrick's head, pushing him toward Big Boi, and he fell to his knees.

"Hey!" Spud shouted at Polo. "Calm the fuck down, man." Spud grabbed a sports jacket off the back of the office chair and tossed it at Fredrick. "Put that on. I don't wanna keep looking at your naked ass."

"Yo, man. Don't ever holler at me again," Polo said.

Slowly, Spud turned his head in Polo's direction. "What?"

"I didn't stutter, nigga. I said . . ." Spud took a step toward him.

"Hey! Hey! Hey!" Big Boi shouted as he stepped between them. "Knock it off!" That was exactly what Fredrick wanted them to do. *Take your time. Keep fucking around. Eventually, the police will come and it would be all over, you black bastards* he thought. When Big Boi was satisfied both had calmed down, he went back over to Fredrick.

"Now, open the safe." After Fredrick put on the jacket, he turned the knob. When the door opened, Polo pushed him away and Big Boi peered inside. There were a few stacks of cash, some jewelry, files, and of course, the black book. Big Boi tossed the cash to Polo then stuck the jewelry in his pocket. Fredrick was exhausted but he watched carefully, hoping they didn't take his black book. Big Boi didn't want him to see him take it. As far as Fredrick knew, it was supposed to be just a random robbery.

Polo peered at Fredrick. "What the fuck are you looking at, peckerwood?" he yelled. He was frustrated because he had to let Spud get away with talking to him like that. He walked up on Fredrick with the gun pointed at his forehead. "Close yo' fuckin' eyes." Fredrick closed them and squeezed them tight.

"Take the money. Just please don't kill me," he begged. Big Boi swiftly tucked the book away in his pants then closed the safe.

"Let's go." Spud snapped his finger at Polo, signaling him to come on before he left the room.

"Be there in a minute . . . Up on your fuckin' knees." Polo held the gun on him while he did as he was told. "I want your pretty, rich, white ass to remember this every time you go to thinking you have control over the black man. You hear me?" Fredrick nodded. "Alright." Polo brought the gun down on top of his head, knocking him out.

## 14

"I call," Randy stated as he pushed another two thousand worth of chips toward the dealer. Several businessmen surrounded the table dressed in suits, all on the same mission to beat the house. Two of the players folded their hands but the last man stuck around to see who really had the best hand. "What are you gonna do?" Randy asked.

The man slid another thousand dollars' worth of chips into the pot. "Raising another grand."

Randy smiled then slid in more chips. "And I raise you another five."

The onlookers whistled out loud as the man studied Randy curiously. "You're bluffin'."

Randy shrugged. "You gonna bet or tuck your fuckin' tail?" The man peered at his hand again. They were playing Lowball and he had a seven high but there was a good chance Randy had a five or a six.

"Ugh!" the man grunted and wiped his forehead. "I think I'll fold," he announced regretfully then threw in his cards. "Let me see your hand."

Randy flipped the cards over. He had a pair of nines which was a losing hand. "I bluffed you," Randy said. "Scared men can't win." The crowd couldn't believe it and the man sitting across from him was pissed off.

"Sonofabitch!" A waitress walked over and whispered something in Randy's ear and he nodded. She returned seconds later with a cordless phone in her hand.

"Hello?"

"We have the black book." It was Spud.

"Good. Just for good measure, photocopy every page then bring it to me."

"You got it."

"Hey! How's Polo holding up?"

"I don't know where you got that clown." Randy chuckled.

"Lighten up. He's a handful but I trust him." He hung up. "Deal me in. I just made two million dollars."

"Your bet, Mr. Harris," the dealer confirmed. The waitress interrupted him again by tapping him on the shoulder.

"What is it, now?" he said with frustration. "Can't you see I'm gambling?" She whispered into his ear again and Randy peered over her shoulder toward the lounge. Jenny was sitting on a sofa with her legs crossed, looking elegant in a red wraparound dress. She held up two glasses, motioning for him to come join her. "Uhhh . . . why don't you just cash me out?" Randy slid his rack of chips to her and rose from his seat. "I'll pick my money up later." A handsome white man that looked about thirty years of age was sitting next to Jenny when Randy arrived.

Randy grunted but the gentleman ignored him so Randy tapped him on the shoulder. "She's with me."

The guy took offense. "And just who the fuck are you?"

Fiddling with his cufflinks, Randy smirked. "You got about ten seconds to move your ass before you get fucked up." The man jumped up with anger in his face. Randy grabbed the collar of his jacket and slung him over the glass table next to theirs. Drinks spattered on the floor as security rushed to his aid. "I'm okay." He glared at the man getting up on his knees. "Go over to the bar and get yourself another drink. On me." He sat down next to Jenny. "You rang?"

Jenny finished sipping from her brandy glass. She seemed unimpressed by his heroic act of violence. "I did."

"Why?"

"Because I wanted to have a drink with you." Randy picked up his glass and sniffed the rim.

"Mm, Brandy."

"You know your stuff. I was thinking a thug like you might say it was something cheap like . . . Christian Brothers."

"A thug like me?" He peered down at his shirt and tie. "You know this suit I'm wearing is by Steve Harvey? Custom-made cufflinks." He took off his shoe and showed her the inside.

"Specially made for Randy Harris," Jenny read. "Cute."

"Cute hell, that's class." Randy put his shoe back on. "I left that thug shit back in the joint."

"I bet your daughter would be proud." Jenny sipped her drink. While she let her eyes roam The Den, Randy stared at the side of her head.

"Well I can see where this conversation is going." He stood. "Excuse me." Jenny clutched his hand, pulling him back onto the sofa. She wrapped her leg around him and kissed him on the lips. Seconds later she came up for air.

"Let's get out of here, baby," she whispered seductively. She stood while still holding his hand. "Let's go."

"Okay. Let's stop and get some of that weed you like to smoke," he said. As they passed the bar, Randy spotted a familiar-looking woman sitting at the end of the bar. She was looking straight ahead, ignoring the drink in front of her. Though he could only see the side of her face, he was sure he knew her from somewhere. Subconsciously, he started for the bar, but Jenny intervened by tugging his arm the other way. Seeing Jenny from the rear cleared his mind of the woman. He happily followed her out the exit. The woman finally turned her head when he was gone. She smiled to herself before taking a drink.

Hours later Randy awoke in his bedroom. He looked next to him but Jenny wasn't there. His lips were chapped and his throat was dry, just like the last time. As usual with Jenny, he didn't remember a thing that happened the night before. He rolled over and sat up on the edge of the bed. After wiping the sleep from his eyes, he saw what was left of the joint he and Jenny smoked sitting in the ashtray. Curiously, he picked it up and examined the wrapping. It seemed to be wrapped in regular rolling paper but he had to be sure it was weed he was smoking. Slowly, he began to unravel it as a shadow came over him. Randy turned his head to find Jenny standing there. She had her mouth twisted in a wicked sneer and held a butcher's knife in her hand.

"Being a bit too nosy for your own good," she growled then raised the knife.

"Jenny, no!" Randy screamed. He raised his hands to try to block the knife but woke up panting in a cold sweat. Randy peered to the left then to the right while he tried to collect himself. When he realized it was just a dream, he reached for his cigarettes on the nightstand. Quickly, he retracted his hand after he saw the butt of the joint sitting in the ashtray. This time it was real. He looked down at Jenny who was sleeping soundly with her face under the pillow. Randy contemplated searching the guts of the joint but the thought alone sent a chill down his spine.

The buzzer to the front gate went off so Randy got up and slipped into his robe and slippers on the way to the living room. He looked at the security screens on the TV. He saw Spud's face and buzzed him in. Randy was standing by the counter fixing a pot of coffee while he watched the news on TV when Spud walked in the kitchen and dropped the mail on the table.

"How many?" Randy asked as he poured two cups of coffee. Spud held up three fingers. Randy dropped three cubes of sugar into his cup then set it on the table in front of him. When Randy took a seat next to him, Spud slid him the black book and the photocopies. The pages were filled with a lot of business he didn't understand. After about ten minutes, he shook his head. "Morgen's a slick bastard." He rose from the table and led Spud back to his office then opened a cabinet, revealing a safe. He took out a briefcase and handed it to Spud. "That's six hundred thousand dollars in cash," Randy explained. "You, Polo's, and Big Boi's half of the million split. I'll pay Yandy myself." Randy took a seat in his office chair. "How is she anyway?"

Jenny crept into the kitchen and her eyes locked on the black book sitting on the table. She glanced in both directions before she tiptoed closer to the table. After careful examination, she realized the book was of no interest to her so she left the room. Outside Randy's office door, she heard voices.

"She misses you and is waiting on you to call her with some kind of explanation for what happened that night you just up and left her," Spud said.

Randy's elbows rested on the arms of his chair while he clasped his fingers together. "I'ma have my secretary schedule us a trip somewhere to make it up to her. I love Yandy. We were just friends for so long that I kinda overlook her, you know what I'm saying?"

"No," Spud said plainly. "While we're just talking, when are we gonna start seeing some revenue from this hotel?"

Randy's gaze shifted to the floor. "I've been meaning to talk to y'all about that."

That did not sound good to Spud. "I'm listening."

Randy took a deep breath. "I'ma buy out the crew except for you."

Spud's eyebrows shot up. "For how much?"

Randy shrugged. "Say . . . a million each."

"And if they refuse?"

"They won't have a choice."

He reclined in his chair. "And me?"

Randy looked him in the eye. "You'd assume the position as my right-hand man. Same as the old days."

Spud scowled. "What?" He jumped up, planted his hands on the desk, and leaned forward. "Is that what you think of me? As your fuckin' right-hand man? A little buddy?"

"Calm down."

"No, you calm down. I'm fuckin' thirty-nine years old. We ain't kids no more!" Spud's eyes narrowed as he shook his index finger at Randy. "You're a fuckin' no good piece of shit, you know that?"

"Look who's tal—"

"Sixteen years ago I would have went for that bullshit, but now . . . I'm smart enough to see that Randy Harris is all about Randy Harris, and everybody else comes after." He snatched his briefcase up and stormed to the door. He stopped suddenly and turned around. "By the way, you can cash me out too. I ain't like you, I'm not selling out my fuckin' friends."

"Like AJ? He was your friend, wasn't he? You killed him because he was late," Randy shouted.

"He knew the rules."

"Yeah, he knew the rules, and you knew mine." Randy fired up a cigarette.

"I guess there's nothing else to be said." Randy shrugged and Spud walked out the door. Jenny ducked into the next room, just missing Spud storm out Randy's office.

Randy stood, unfazed by what had just taken place. He walked back to the kitchen, sat at the table, sipped his coffee, and sorted through the mail. He came across another letter addressed to him with no return address. After taking a short breath, he opened it. Inside was a picture of a little girl.

She had two long ponytails on either side of her head and her wide smile revealed two missing front teeth. From the looks of her attire and the scenery, she was either going to or coming from church. On the back was his daughter's name, Tiffany, and her age was nine. A smirk crept on his face as he traced the photo with his finger. Jenny watched him from the doorway. He closed his eyes, imagining what she would look like as a grown woman. Probably in college somewhere or with kids on welfare, living on Section 8. If she was, he was to blame because of the bad example he set as a father.

His mind traveled back to that familiar woman he saw sitting at the bar. Now that he thought about it, he had seen her out in the parking lot earlier that day. She was sitting in a black Volvo just staring at him. Could it be? No, it couldn't. The woman was too old, way too old to be his daughter. *Then who is it?* he thought. When Randy finally opened his eyes, he saw Jenny standing beside him with concern all over her face.

"Who's that?" Jenny asked. She took the photo from his hand. "Pretty. Looks kinda like you."

"My daughter. Her name is Tiffany." His voice was low as Jenny sat.

"When did you—" Randy got up and walked away. Minutes later, Jenny heard Randy playing the piano in the living room. While he played, he sang Ray Charles' "Drown in My Own Tears." Jenny stared at the picture of the little girl and wondered what was going through Randy's mind when he threatened to kill her. After Randy told her what happened years ago, that night he was arrested, she really didn't know what to think of him. Was he a gruesome murderer who would've killed his own seed over some money? Or was he just a man stuck, trying to be somebody fearsome and scarcely respected?

"Your past is who you are," she said to herself. Randy was deep into the song when Jenny entered the living room. He was singing toward the window but his eyes were closed. Slowly, she crept behind him and placed her hands on his shoulders. He opened his eyes but didn't stop playing. Music soothed his soul, and at the moment, his soul was aching. Jenny whispered something in his ear that he didn't understand.

"What?" he asked.

This time Jenny yelled, "Will ... you ... marry ... meee?" Immediately, he stopped playing the piano. When he stood and faced her, he wore the biggest smile was on his face.

"What did you say?"

Jenny peered down at the floor then back up at him. "I said, will you marry me?"

"Yes!"

"Do you promise to take care of me? To beat me when I've been bad? To shower me with exotic gifts? Do you vow to love me no matter how bad I've been or how many times I mess up with you? Huh, Mr. Harris?"

Randy held both of her hands. "I promise."

"Then it shall happen. In return, you shall have," she turned around and showcased herself, "all of this at your disposal." Randy was so excited he leapt over the bench, took her down to the floor, and kissed all over her face. "Your first thing on the 'to do' list is to inform Yandy about our engagement then go out and buy me the biggest diamond you can find."

# 15

"Why am I down here?" Fredrick asked. "I already told your fellow officers everything I know."

Madison sat at the table inside the police station across from Fredrick. "I know, Mister. We just wanna go over a few things for our investigation, maybe show you a few photographs."

"I didn't see their faces."

"We know that. We were just trying to see if you could match a voice or two with some faces, you know? Kinda help us get on the right track. Are we clear on that?" Fredrick swallowed.

"Yes."

"Good." He shuffled through some papers. "You say there were three suspects?"

"Yes."

"All male?"

"Yes, well ..."

"Well what? Were the attackers all male or not, Mr. Fredrick?"

Fredrick seemed unsure. "Yes, it was three males."

"You're sure?"

"Yes, I'm sure."

"You're not holding back or leaving anything out?"

"No."

"Now, with all your cameras and security gates, how did they get in?"

"Like I said before, they took my butler, my driver, hostage."

Madison removed his glasses. "They took your driver hostage without you seeing them? See, that's what gets me. Tell me," he licked his lips, "how was that possible?"

Fredrick sighed. "It must have happened when I went in the store."

"Where you met the woman?"

"Yes."

"Tell me about her." He smacked his gum.

"Nothing to tell. I picked her up . . . no, wait . . . she followed me home."

"Your idea or hers?"

Fredrick shrugged. "I don't know. Anyway, I took her to my house. We were about to make love and then those punks came bustin' in."

"And she got away?"

"Yes."

Madison smiled. "She did call us, Fredrick. At least, some woman did. She phoned us from a nearby phone." He shifted in his seat. "The problem is we think whoever this mystery lady is was in on it. She set you up, and you went for it." Fredrick looked surprised. "See, you were too out of it to remember when or what time all this took place, but if you could, I'd bet we'd find it took her enough time for them to clear out before she phoned us." He shook his head and smacked his gum while staring at Fredrick. The door opened and a young, bald-headed, army-built policeman stepped in. He carried a file in his hand. "What is it?" Madison inquired.

"I got the file you wanted, sir." He placed the folder on the table in front of Madison, and Madison carefully examined the file on Spud's crew. He was halfway through it before he reached something that should not have been there.

"Mr. Boyd," Madison said slowly. "I thought we didn't have a file on the woman."

"I never said that."

"Then who . . ." Madison caught himself as the answer to his own question popped in his head. He looked over the complete file of Yandy. She had been busted for several misdemeanors and domestic violence cases. There were other things on paper about her but nothing of interest to Madison. There was also a photograph. Madison examined it then passed it to Fredrick.

"Was that the woman you took home with you?"

Fredrick's angry facial expression said it before he even answered the question. "Yes, it's her."

"I thought so. Ms. Yandy," he said to himself.

"You gonna go pick her up? They stole some very valuable information from me."

Madison rubbed his face. "Unfortunately, that's all we can do. Pick her up and put some pressure on her, but she won't confess because she's good at what she does." He looked over at Boyd. "Show Mr. Fredrick here to the door, will you? And send Law in, please."

Fredrick stood. "That's all?"

"For now." Madison stood and shook his hand. When Fredrick left, he rolled up his sleeves and loosened his tie. The second Law walked through the door, Madison grabbed him and slung him over the table. Paperwork flew everywhere. Law covered his head as he fell to the floor.

"Jesus, Madison!" Law hollered.

"Get up! Get up, you piece of shit." Madison lifted him by his shirt then pushed him into the wall. He clutched his face with his hand. "Look at me! Why did you lie to me?"

"I didn't." His voice was weak. "What are you—"

"You didn't? You didn't tell me that we didn't have a file on the girl in Spud's crew?" He yanked his shirt. "Look at me and tell me you didn't say that."

"Yeah, yeah. I said it, Madison." Law looked afraid.

"Why?" Madison yelled. "Why did you tell me that when I just got finished going over a complete file on her?"

"I promise, I searched the entire file and didn't see anything on the girl. Somebody messed up, but it wasn't me." Madison stared into his eyes and saw sincerity. This was his longtime friend and he didn't want to believe that he would lie to him.

"Somebody did." Madison released him then turned, heading for the door. "C'mon, let's see if we can find this broad."

"May I help you?" Yandy was sitting on the terrace of the hotel's restaurant, staring out at the highway. She was deep in thought until the waitress appeared and interrupted her.

"Excuse me?" Yandy asked.

"Can I get you something while you wait?"

"Yes, I'm sorry. Umm . . . I'll have a Texas margarita. And could you bring me The Call paper, please? Thanks." Randy walked through the restaurant at a fast pace. He was supposed to meet Yandy there fifteen minutes ago, but unfortunately, he got tied up in a meeting with his investors. He spotted her sitting on the terrace looking down at the highway as her hair blew with the wind. He stopped short of her, admiring her from the distance. She wore a dress, stilettos, and a pair of dark shades. Every so often, she would take a sip from her drink then politely set it back down. Now there's a woman Randy thought to himself. Tender, feminine and submissive. Nothing like Jenny. She was completely the opposite. Jenny was a wildcat that teased just for the thrill of being chased. That was what turned him on about her. When it came to the tug-of-war between Jenny and Yandy, Jenny always won. Yandy was reading her newspaper when she heard Randy grunting.

She peered up and saw him standing over her. "Well hello," she said with a pleasant smile and removed her shades. "Have a seat." Randy set his briefcase in one of the four chairs then took the seat across from her. He motioned for the waitress then ordered a cup of coffee. Yandy touched his hand. "You know . . . the last time we were together we had just had some great make-up sex. Then I went to the shower but when I returned to find you . . . you were gone."

"I can—"

"Before you do, there's more." Her face turned angry. "I answered your office phone and some tramp asked me had you left yet," she smirked embarrassingly as she held back tears. "Can you imagine how that made me feel, Randy? I mean, can you really imagine it? I loved you!"

"Loved?"

Yandy nodded her head. "You know, I was foolish enough to think that jail had changed you but it didn't. You're the same old piece of shit you were when you left, only you're not as young." Yandy fired up a cigarette. "Why are we here?" Randy hesitated. What he was about to say was going to make all the things she'd just said about him seem true. The waitress brought his coffee.

"Here you go, Mr. Harris."

"Thank you." He blew at the hot liquid before he took a sip, allowing enough time for Yandy to calm down.

"So?" she asked impatiently. Randy opened the briefcase, took out a cashier's check for a million dollars, and slid it to her. Yandy picked it up and read it. As soon as she saw the figure her eyebrows shot up. "What's this?"

Randy sat his cup down. "I'm cashing you out. You're no longer a part of the hotel business," he calmly stated, as if what he was doing didn't faze him. She put the check inside her bag.

"You want it all for yourself, don't you, Randy?" She forced a smile as she shook her head in disgust. "What is it with you, man? Are you so stuck on yourself that you feel like you always need total control over everything?"

"Listen, Yandy. You, Spud, Big Boi, and Chuck are still in the business of stealing. Me, I got to separate myself from y'all, and whatever y'all are doing. I got plans, big and legitimate plans. I don't need y'all fuckin' it up by bringing the heat around me." He sat back in his seat. "There it is, I said it. You, Spud or anybody don't like it, I don't give a fuck."

"You're right, you said it, you arrogant bastard!" she hollered as she stood and gathered her things. "And you've done it 'cause I've had it with your black ass." She leaned over the table and said, "Hell hath no fury like a woman scorned." After she straightened her dress, she started walking away.

"One more thing," Randy said. Yandy stopped but did not turn around. "I'm getting married to Jenny." Yandy stood erect for a moment, clutching her bag tightly to hold back her words. After she calmed down a bit, she politely walked away. Randy giggled quietly, knowing that he had stabbed a dagger right through the center of her heart. Then he drank his coffee as the phone rung. "It's Fredrick."

Yandy stormed outside to her truck, fumbling through everything in her purse as she looked for her car keys. While she was doing so, Madison whipped the Crown Victoria into the lot and Law pointed in her direction.

"There!" Madison brought the car to an abrupt stop in front of hers then the two of them jumped out. Yandy froze after she saw them walking toward her while flashing badges.

"Evening, Yandy," Madison said with a smile. "I'm Detective Madison," he looked back at Law, "and this here is my partner, Detective Robert Law."

"Un huh." Yandy hoped they couldn't see the fear in her eyes through her glasses.

"Well, Miss Yandy, we had a forced entry that occurred a few days ago and your name came up."

"Really?"

"That's right," he sang. "The victim told us he was with you when it happened." She stared at him for a moment, wondering how they identified her. "Yandy?"

"Yes. Um, yes, I was there," she admitted.

"And you were the mysterious woman who called us, I presume?"

"Yes, I was."

"Good." He grabbed her arm. "We'd like to ask you a few questions, downtown."

Yandy sighed. "I don't need this shit."

"Yeah, neither do we," Madison replied. "But somebody's gotta do it. C'mon, you can ride with us." Yandy glanced at Randy's office window before she was placed in the backseat of the car. They were pulling out of the lot when Randy walked out the front door.

Randy jumped in his Cadillac and burned rubber out of the parking lot. Northbound, he hit the highway on his way to the park. Some of the people jogged, some power walked around the huge track, but for the most part, the park was empty. It was windy out, not cold but not particularly warm either. Randy circled the area until he found Fredrick's Benz then parked beside it. There was a sign on his windshield.

### By the swings

He buttoned his jacket then took the long stroll around the track until he reached the swings. Fredrick was laughing while he stood next to his daughter who was flying a kite. His son was only a few feet away, teaching their German Shepherd how to catch a tennis ball. Fredrick heard leaves crackling and looked around. Instead of interrupting their fun, Randy nodded then took a seat on a nearby bench.

"Sammy," Fredrick called his son. "Come over here and help your sister."

Sammy frowned. "Ah, dad," he pouted.

"Now, mister!"

"Okay." With his hands in the pockets of his slacks, Fredrick walked over and sat next to Randy. Two squirrels were fighting over an acorn and had Randy's full attention. He liked to see a good squabble.

"What do you know about a woman named Yandy?" Fredrick asked. Randy tried to read Fredrick's blank facial expression to see where he was coming
from.

"Why?" Fredrick lit a cigarette and smoked about half of it then tossed it into the grass.

"My home was robbed the other day and some very important information was taken," Fredrick explained. "Now, as far as I know, they don't have a clue as to what they have," he shrugged. "What I'm trying to say is, I need that book back." His tone was serious.

"What can I do?" "Ask around. Put some people on the streets. Use your clout and spread some cash around. Whatever it takes, just please try to locate it for me."

"How much is it worth to you? Assuming I locate it. And need I remind you, Freddy, you're not talking to a child here so don't hold back on me." Fredrick gazed at his two happy children. Sammy had tackled his sister and the dog had tackled him.

"Seven figures.

"I'll see what I can do." That was enough to temporarily put Fredrick's mind at ease. He stood then went back to join his family.

"Hey, Fred," Randy called. Fredrick stopped and turned around. "You think I was involved somehow, don't you?"

"Truthfully?" Fredrick looked down at the grass for a second then back to Randy. "Yes." Randy heard little Sammy ask his dad if the scars on his face hurt. For some reason, Randy thought he should have felt pity for the family, the businessman, but he didn't.

The sun was setting and a collage of yellow, orange, and blue covered the sky. It was cool outside and the evening air chilled Randy's dome as he speeded down the highway to a meeting with Morgen. Girls were riding by him honking their horns, waving and checking out his expensive car. On another day he would have been enticed by all the attention, but at the moment, his head was in another place. *Where did Fredrick learn Yandy's name?* Randy wondered. More importantly, was she also one of the suspects that Fredrick was thinking of? Randy had come up with a lot of great schemes in the past but this time he believed he might have screwed up. He shouldn't have involved Yandy. Not only could Fredrick identify her, but she could also be linked to him. Randy jumped into the right lane and got off on the exit. From the highway, he could see Morgen's Lincoln parked under the bridge with its flashers on. He pulled alongside the road behind Morgen's car. Morgen got out and ran to Randy's car.

"Where is it?" he asked nervously. Randy showed it to him but when he went to reach for it Randy snatched it back.

"Not so fast," Randy said. A look of confusion fell over Morgen's face.

"What's the problem, brother?" Randy grunted.

"Brother, huh? White people always want to act like family when they're trying to beat a nigga." Morgen was baffled.

"Randy, I don't understand."

"Understand this, the price just went up." Through suspicious eyes, Morgen watched him.

"Who've you been talking to about this?" Randy gazed out the window at the passing cars.

"Fredrick offered me two million dollars to buy it back," he lied. Morgen's mouth fell open.

"Jesus! He knows?"

"No, just wants me to put my ear to the streets and see what I can find out." Morgen began rubbing the gold ring on his finger.

"I can probably go as high as two and a half million but that's it."

"I was thinking more like three." Randy opened his door. "I'ma take a piss while you think it over." Morgen noticed Randy had left the black book on the seat and he gazed at it with greed in his eyes. *If I only had a gun, I would . . .*

"Forgot something," Randy said as he opened the door and picked up the book.

"Conniving black bastard," Morgen spat. By the time Randy got back inside the car, Morgen had made up his mind. "Okay, you win. Three million. But it'll take me about a week to get the money."

"Fine by me. Long as I get it." Randy wiped the book down with his handkerchief before he handed it over.

## 16

A month later Randy and Jenny were married on a secluded island in Port Antonio, Jamaica. Randy rented an eight-bedroom beachfront home that lodged all twenty of his guests and an eight-man staff to wait on them hand and foot. Ginuwine sang at the reception while the happy couple danced for the first time but the real excitement was Randy's his and hers gift. After the vows were exchanged, Randy led his new bride to the front of the home where two brand new Porsche 996 Turbos were parked. One was fire engine red and the other was platinum gray. Jenny kicked off her shoes and straddled the front seat of the red one as Randy got into the gray one. The two raced around the beautiful coast enjoying the scenery as well as the ride. Jenny was shocked to see all the goats and chickens running wild like regular pets. While the exotic island fascinated her, Randy zoomed right past. She took the challenge and shifted gears, causing dust to blow from under her tires.

Randy held the lead around the bend, hogging both lanes so Jenny couldn't pass. Dirt covered her front windshield and forced her to slow down. By the time she caught up, Randy had parked, gotten out, and was peering out at the ocean waters. Six white women in bikinis were enjoying a game of volleyball on the beach while some people were scattered about trying to catch an authentic tan and others played in the water. Randy turned to face her and Jenny's dress blew sideways as she walked to him. For what seemed like an eternity, they stared into each other's eyes then they shared a long, passionate kiss.

"It's beautiful, isn't it?" Randy said. He leaned against the car while Jenny stood between his legs.

"It sure is," she smiled. "I've dreamed of seeing places like this since I was a child." The sweet scent on Jenny's neck soothed Randy's nostrils. Gently, he caressed her neck with his nose. She closed her eyes and cocked her head back, enjoying the feeling. Before she knew it, Randy had unwrapped her dress and let it blow away. She stood there wearing nothing but her bra, thong, and garter belt. Jenny faced him and giggled shyly.

"Baby, what are you doing?"

"Let's go at it right here in front of everybody," Randy dared. Jenny leaned in and kissed his nose.

"Let's save the kinky stuff for tonight, okay?" She faced the beach. "Right now, I just wanna enjoy the moment." They fell silent, each in their own thoughts before Randy wrapped his arms around her shoulders.

"From now on, I'm gonna take care of you. Daddy's gonna buy you a mockingbird if you want it."

Jenny kissed his hand. "All I want out of life is what I got coming. Nothing more, nothing less." Out the front seat, Randy picked up a bottle of champagne and two glasses, and Jenny held the glasses while he popped the cork. The liquid erupted all over the hood of the car. She shook the hair out of her face while Randy filled the glasses.

"I'd like to propose a toast," he announced, holding his glass out in front of him. "From rags to riches. May our lives be filled with joy while we make bittersweet memories. Cheers." After they tapped their glasses together, they downed the chilled liquid then tossed the glasses out onto the road. "Let's go," Randy said. "Last one back don't get no head tonight."

"Bet." Jenny started her engine. "Randy!" she yelled through the open window.

"What?"

"Watch out for the glass in front of your tire." She laughed as she burned rubber, making her tires spray dust all over his windshield. Randy looked down at the broken glass near his tires. Jenny had done him again. He could do nothing but shake his head.

That night, Randy chartered a hundred and fifty-six-foot yacht. Among the guests were Jenny's crew, Karl from the governor's office, Polo, and of course, the host himself. While countless bottles of bubbly were being popped, the girls pranced around in bathing suits that left little to the imagination. Karl was high off blow and hyper as a sixteen-year-old-boy. Polo grinded behind Jenny in the middle of the deck, dancing to the music. Jenny was drunk and seemed to have forgotten that Polo wasn't Randy.

She allowed his hands to violate her body like he was the rightful owner. Randy stood on the upper deck in his robe with a champagne glass in his hand, staring out at the ocean. Life was truly great for a change. Never once while locked up did he imagine he would go this far in life, especially as old as he was. He was enjoying his drink when RiRi walked up behind him. She placed her hands on his shoulders and massaged them gently.

"Guess who?" He could smell the alcohol on her breath.

"I know it's not my baby," he replied. RiRi reached around into his robe and grabbed his dick. Randy removed her hand as he spun around. "Damn, girl, it's my wedding night. Show some respect."

"It's not like I haven't already fucked you," she reminded him. "Don't worry. Jenny won't get upset, I promise." She placed her hands on his chest and opened his robe. He rested against the railing while her tongue tickled his nipples. Slowly, she fell to her knees. Randy's leg trembled nervously when she reached her cold hand inside his boxers and pulled out his dick. RiRi sucked on it for about ten seconds before he pushed her face back and stepped away. She wiped slobber from around her lips with the back of her hand then glared up at him. "This is a party. What the hell is wrong with you?" she questioned as she got up from her knees.

"My wife is down there, RiRi," he said while pointing toward the stairs leading to the lower level.

"Let me show you something." RiRi took his hand and quietly led him down the small stairwell and onto the main deck. She pointed to a glass cased cabin where another party of sorts was going on. As they walked into the cabin, the lights were dimmed and seductive music played as they witnessed Polo leaning against the wet bar while Jenny danced erotically before his eyes. Her bra had been removed. Karl was stretched out on a plush off-white lounge chair with his tie wrapped around his neck like a noose while Freeda performed a lap dance. Sasha walked around with her camera, filming it all. When she spotted RiRi's face in the camera, she saw RiRi signaling for her to come. "This is how we get down, Randy," RiRi explained while she waited for Sasha. "You're gonna have to get with the program."

Jenny removed her panties and bent over, jiggling her ass in Polo's face. Polo ran his tongue up her ass crack, and Randy had seen enough. His anger had gotten the best of him. He took a step in their direction but RiRi held him back.

"No, sir, let her be. I promise they won't do any more than what they're doing now. Okay?" She nodded toward the chaise sitting in the corner. "Go over there and make yourself comfortable. Sasha and I will join you shortly." Randy glared at Jenny who seemed to be enjoying herself. *Fuck it* he thought. *I'll play their little games.* When he turned and headed for the chaise, Jenny cut her eyes at him and smirked. Randy slipped into the bathroom and fished around the pocket of his robe until he located what he was looking for. The little purple pill he had gotten hookup on. He swallowed handfuls of water to wash it down. He had heard Viagra worked and he was going to put it to the test. When he came out, RiRi was laying on the chaise with her legs agape while Sasha lay next to her, three fingers deep inside her pussy. RiRi enjoyed playing with her own nipples while watching Sasha penetrate her. Randy stood at the head of the chaise with his dick sticking up.

"Who's first?"

RiRi smiled. "Me." She positioned herself on all fours and waited on him to enter her. "Stick it in my culo." Sasha spit slobber down RiRi's ass crack then smeared it around her booty hole. Randy spread her cheeks wide, then ever so gently, entered her.

"Uhh! Uhh!" RiRi moaned as she gripped the cherry wood of the chaise. "Hit it good, papi!" Randy clutched her tiny waist, bringing her body back hard against his. RiRi reached back between her legs and rubbed her clit while he continuously stabbed her. Sasha eased away and picked up the camera then stood behind Randy, filming his ass muscles tighten with each stroke. "Ooh, spank me!" RiRi begged. "Call me Jenny." Randy smacked her on the ass. "Oww!" she screamed. He clutched the back of her neck, choking her.

"Please! Please! Don't hurt me, please! Stop it, daddy!"

He stopped. "You alright?"

RiRi peered back at him through wild eyes like he was stupid. "Don't pay any attention to my speech. Now hit it and talk to me like a bitch."

Randy started stroking her again. "You like that, bitch? Huh, Jenny? You triflin' whore." "I'm sorry! I'm sorry! Stop it! Stop it!" Sasha had filmed enough. Her pussy juice started oozing down her thigh. Watching RiRi get abused like that got her aroused. Her anus was throbbing and aching to be plugged. She sat the camera down, then took position next to RiRi.

"Help me out, RiRi." RiRi licked her fingers and rubbed them across Sasha's asshole. Randy withdrew himself from RiRi and entered Sasha. She screamed out as every inch of him slowly dug into her insides. She closed her eyes and bit down on her bottom lip before letting out a loud howl when he hit the bottom.

"Owww! Pull it out! Pull it out!" Randy continued ramming her unmercifully. For about forty-five minutes, he went back and forth, from girl to girl, splitting their asses like logs and busting nuts. When he collapsed on the bed panting, Sasha showed up with a joint. He had been craving some of that weed all month. She inhaled and hit him with three shotgun blasts, nearly busting his chest. That intense feeling came back to him again. He was so high he thought he had reached the limit. Then like a thief in the night the high vanished just as quick as it came. Sweat rolled down his forehead while he sat up on the chaise between the two girls. Though his eyes were barely open, he thought he saw Jenny bent over the bar while Polo long-dicked her. Randy shook it off thinking it was just the drugs and liquor that had him paranoid. He was not seeing his wife over there getting knocked by his goon.

"Gimme some more of that shit," he begged. Sasha lit another one. This time he snatched it from her and smoked it himself. Several minutes later his head started bobbing around. It leaned to the left then to the right. Randy glanced up and saw Jenny standing before him, naked with a wicked smirk on her face. He smiled at her then his face fell forward into the chaise. The girls offered to let Polo hit the joint but he declined.

"I don't smoke nothing that I didn't see get rolled. I been in the joint and I know better than to accept everything that's offered to me."

Sasha stood over him naked with her hands on her hips. "What're you saying, Polo?"

Polo snorted. "It's really self-explanatory. Everythang that glitters ain't gold. Young, funky cock hoes can't make me do shit I don't want to do."

Sasha looked over at RiRi who was standing next to her. "Booty bandit?"

Nodding her head, RiRi said, "Being locked up for so long? Yes, I would say so."

Sasha, using her index finger said, "C'mere, Polo." Thirty minutes and a shot of butt later Polo was knocked out on the floor. A victim of the same joint that put Randy on his ass.

The unsettled waves rocking the yacht awakened Randy. He blinked his eyes repeatedly and looked around. He was now in another cabin and in a bed. He looked over to his left and saw Jenny sound asleep. As he got up to retrieve his robe, the constant motion made his stomach uneasy. When he walked out of the cabin and onto the main deck, he saw Polo asleep on the chaise lounge where he, RiRi, and Sasha were just hours earlier. What was interesting was that everything was as clean as a whistle but his head was pounding like he had been partying all night. Female chatter could be heard coming from the deck above. He gingerly walked up the stairs and saw Sasha and RiRi sitting at the table eating breakfast. RiRi had on the captain's personal hat.

"Mornin', sleepy head," Sasha said.

"Mornin', papi." Randy waved. He was about to ask about Karl until he looked overboard and saw him swimming in the ocean with Freeda. Naked. It was something peculiar about the way the girls were staring at him. It alerted him that something wild had gone on the night before but he couldn't remember a damned thing.

## 17

"The cops brought me in for questioning a month ago," Yandy said. She was pacing around Spud's living room floor with her shoes off. "Did you know that?" Spud nodded. He was slouched on the couch, still groggy from being awakened so early. Half a cup of coffee was sitting on the table in front of him waiting to be finished. After about two of them, he would be ready to begin his day. Yandy's eyes narrowed on him. "You knew and didn't bother to see what happened?"

Spud cleared his throat. "Honestly, I panicked, Yandy. When I found out that you had been brought in, I got the hell outta dodge and hopped on the first plane to Belize."

"Belize?"

"Yeah, it's nice over there. You should see it. They have these—"

"Okay, okay," she interrupted with frustration. "They don't know who you three are, and they don't have nothing on me, other than I was there. They were just fishing, hoping I'd crack under pressure."

"That wasn't supposed to happen. What happened to—" Yandy raised her hand, shushing him.

"Let me handle that. I'll talk to him."

Spud thought momentarily. "You know Randy bought me out?"

"That's just like that pig. Bastard gave me a check for a million dollars then sent me on my way. Right before he told me he was engaged." As she stared out the window, she felt Spud's body heat when he crept up behind her. His nose barely came to her shoulder but she remained still while he inhaled her scent. Her body tensed when she felt his hand caress her butt. "Spud?"

"Huh?" He continued fondling her.

"What're you doing?"

"Honestly." He kissed her shoulders. "Tryin' to fuck." Yandy's body unintentionally relaxed as her eyes closed while he kissed the back of her neck.

"Why . . . mmm . . . why are you . . . tryin' to fuck me? Huh?" He removed the belt from her dress and pulled it down to her ankles. Spud had to take a step back to admire her natural beauty for a moment. She posed with her hands on her hips, flossing her peach colored fishnet panty set as her curly pubic hairs protruded through the holes. Spud shucked off his robe, and Yandy gazed down at the little man standing there with his dick straining to bust out his briefs. She had to smile.

"Spud, I'll break your little body in half. Look at me." She ran her hands over her body. "I'm a lot of woman." He pulled down his drawers and his long ten-inch dick sprang up then bobbed like a diving board. The look on her face showed she was impressed by the size of his sex weapon.

"I'm a whole lot of man," Spud bragged. "To the bat cave."

After Yandy removed her clothing, she relaxed in his soft bed and Spud climbed on top. When she spread her creamy thighs, Spud caught an eyeful of her pink vulva. He shot nut all over her legs and stomach.

"Nooooo," Yandy hollered angrily. "Get up! Get the fuck up!"

"Wait a minute," Spud pleaded.

"Nah, I knew this wouldn't work." Yandy jumped up and raced to the bathroom. Spud hit the mattress, angry at himself for blowing a once in a lifetime chance. When Yandy returned from the bathroom,

Spud was standing out on the front porch smoking a cigarette. He heard her step out the front door.

"Was it good for you as it was for me?" he said jokingly. Yandy couldn't help but laugh and he joined her. Now that it was over, the shit was funny to them.

"I can't believe you shot cum all over me before you got to get inside," she said.

"Me neither." After the laughter died down, he passed her the cigarette and became serious. "What are we gonna do about our old buddy Randy?" Yandy tossed the cigarette as she turned to face him.

"Bring his bigheaded ass back down to earth and relieve him of his money." She offered him her hand. "You down?"

He shook it. "Retaliation is a must where we come from." Yandy kissed him gently then held his cheeks with her hands.

"Still friends?"

"I guess so."

Yandy chuckled. "Call me later."

While she was walking to her truck, Spud yelled, "You missed out on a great lay."

Law continuously snapped photographs of Spud and Yandy on the porch as they were shaking hands.

"Can you read their lips?" Madison asked.

"Ahh, whatever she just said, it looks like he agreed to it."

"Um hm. They're planning something. I can feel it." He inhaled his cigarette. "The question is what?"

Law shrugged. "It's probably nothing."

"Maybe it's everything," Madison retorted in full disagreement with his partner. "First she's in cahoots with Morgen. Profits at his hotel go down then she introduces him to Randy. They set up the bank robberies, now they're in business together. Trouble is, Randy is a greedy bastard. He breaks the deal by probably forcing them to cash out. Now these two are fucking each other and no doubt plotting revenge."

"How you figure all that, Madison?"

"Because I'm a seasoned veteran. I've been around and interrogated a lot of snitches. These kinds of thoughts come natural. I'm telling you, Randy's living the glamorous life and smoking cigars with the big fish. Now he don't want to school with the sardines anymore." Yandy planted a kiss on Spud's lips. "Get a shot of that."

"Ah ha!" Law blurted.

"What? What?"

"I just read his lips." He sat the camera down in the seat. "What'd he say?"

"I made out the words, 'you a great lay'."

Madison smiled triumphantly, showing nicotine-stained teeth. He inhaled a deep breath. "You smell that?"

"What? You farted?"

"No. Deceit, my friend. Deceit." Madison started the car. "Let's get outta here."

Karl Peterson, Randy, Morgen, and three representatives from the Save the Kids Foundation all held a mock check for five hundred thousand donated by the hotel. They held their poses for the cameras as Randy maintained a false smile while the bulbs flashed.

*So this is how the politicians do it?* he thought to himself. *Feed the public a bunch of charity bullshit and they love you for it.* The crowd in the room cheered when Morgen announced Randy Harris as the great humanitarian of the city. Randy raised his hand in acknowledgement as the crowd applauded him. Morgen invited him to the podium, and Randy stepped behind it, shaking Morgen's hand in the process. He mouthed the words "thank you" before Morgen left him alone. The crowd quieted down when he spoke into the microphone.

"Thank you. The children are our future so I'm going to do my part to help make sure they get what's coming to them. Higher learning. That means we have to start putting money to the side to invest in schools, books, computers and scholarship funds. Because one day they are going to inherit this place we call earth. And I, for one, don't want to leave it in the hands of a bunch of uneducated minds." The crowd rose to its feet clapping and cheering. As Randy enjoyed the respect, his eyes scanned the room until they fell upon a hole in the crowd. The light held a glare in his eyes so he had to squint to see the face of the only protester in the room. When she saw him looking, she stood so he could get a good look. It was Olivia, sixteen years older. She was frail, her hair looked like a bad weave, and bags were under her eyes but she was dressed accordingly. The years hadn't been good to her and somehow, he knew she blamed him for her fuck ups. Olivia waited for the applause to die down before she opened her mouth to speak.

"Excuse me, Mr. Harris? I have a question," she shouted. Randy licked his lips.

Before he had a chance to decline, Morgen said, "Go right ahead, miss. Mr. Harris has all the time in the world to address the public."

Olivia took three steps forward. "I would just like to know why you are so concerned about every kid in the city's future except for your own?" The cameramen took shots of her and the reporters broke out their pads and pencils. Jenny sat at a table next to the stage regarding Olivia as Randy put on a false smile.

"Ah, miss, I'm sorry but I don't know what you're talking about. Uh, security, could you please show this insane woman to the door, please?" Within seconds, several members of the security team jumped on her, seizing both her arms.

"Tell these people who Randy Harris really is!" Olivia shouted. "Tell 'em how you threatened to kill your own daughter over money!"

"Get her outta here!" Randy yelled angrily. The guards scooped her off her feet and hauled her out the door. Randy peered down at Jenny who returned his stare then she stood and left the room as well. Randy exited the stage leaving Morgen to close the ceremony.

Morgen was so baffled that all he could say to the crowd was, "Thank you." After Randy stormed into his office, he snatched off his jacket then flung it across the room. He stepped outside, gazing down at the security guards escorting Olivia off the property. An idea hit him. Quietly, he went back inside, picked up the phone, and called Polo's cell.

"Hello," Polo answered.

"Where are you?"

"Down in The Den gambling. Man, it's some freaks down here and I'm all over 'em. What's up?"

"Security just escorted a woman out the building. Stop what you're doing and find out where she's going."

"What? Man, didn't you just hear me say it's some freaks down here?"

"Now, Polo!" Randy hung up the phone. Next he called Jenny but didn't receive an answer.

Morgen stormed into Randy's office while he was setting the phone back down. "What the hell was that?" Morgen demanded.

"Did you just walk into my office, Morgen?"

Morgen stopped short of Randy's desk. "Right now there is a group of reporters downstairs waiting for you to come down."

Ignoring him, Randy pointed at the door. "Did you . . . just walk in my fuckin' office . . . without knocking?"

Morgen scowled. "So what? You wouldn't have this office if it weren't for me." Morgen pointed a finger at him. "Don't get bigheaded with me, boy. I'll hang you with the same goddamn rope I'm feeding you." "Boy?" Randy stepped from behind his desk.

"Who the fuck you callin' boy? Is that what you think of me? I'm one of your fuckin' kids?" Randy looked very intimidating in Morgen's face, glaring at him.

Morgen spread his arms wide. "What are you doing? This is for me and you. Bitch comes in and airs your dirty laundry to the public and you take it out on a friend?"

"You're no friend of mine," Randy stated bluntly. The statement took Morgen by surprise. He was at a loss for words as his feelings were hurt.

"I guess there's nothing left to be said." Morgen walked over to the door and opened it. "If you want to apologize, I'll be down in the club having a drink. If you don't," he shrugged, "then I'll be insulted. And I don't take insults kindly, Harris." With that said, he closed the door behind him.

Music blared inside the club. Exotic dancers stood on circular platforms seven feet off the ground while entertaining the crowd. The music was hip-hop, and the crowd was too immature for Morgen but the scenery was worthwhile. Young, black, white, and Hispanic females were in the club getting tipsy and buck wild. Disco lights flashed throughout the room and big-boobed waitresses served the drinks.

Morgen saw a group of black guys occupying the pool tables. He had a pretty good stick so he contemplated walking over and shooting a few games, but he wanted to wait for Randy to come down. He hoped he did because Morgen would hate to have something done to him. He took a seat at the bar across from the dance floor and received a few winks and smiles from some of the women. They could tell he was a wealthy man by his expensive suit.

The waitress placed a napkin before him. "Can I get you something to drink?"

"Yeah. Let me get a dry martini and a glass of whatever it is Mr. Harris drinks." Morgen took out his cigarettes while he waited.

Morgen grew tired of waiting on Randy to show up. After twenty minutes of waiting and two drinks, he made his way to the pool table where the black guys were hanging. He was in the middle of his third game when the waitress walked up on him.

"Mr. Morgen?" the waitress said. Morgen completed the shot before he faced her. The fine black woman standing before him sent a jolt though his scrotum.

"Yes?"

The waitress handed him a martini off her tray. "Complements of the young lady over there." She nodded toward Jenny who was sitting at a booth against the wall. Morgen was confused and didn't know what to make of it. He raised his glass in acceptance, but Jenny patted the seat next to her and motioned for him to come over.

"Gentlemen, if you'd excuse me for a moment," Morgen said. He sat the stick down and made his way through the crowd to where Jenny sat. She patted the seat again and Morgen complied. He jacked his slacks and took a seat. Jenny slid over until their bodies touched.

"Hi, Morgen," Jenny said in a husky voice.

"Hello." She placed her hand on his leg. "Aren't you Randy's new, young, and I must say, very attractive bride?"

"Yes." Jenny shrugged. "So? You got a problem with getting to know me . . . intimately . . . just because I'm married? If so, then I made a bad decision. Sorry." Jenny stood as if she were about to leave but Morgen grabbed her wrist.

"Wait . . . Wait. Have a seat. We're both mature adults, I think we can have a few drinks and enjoy each other's company."

Jenny sat and crossed her leg over his. "Okay." Morgen's phone vibrated and when he dug it out his inside pocket and checked the LCD screen Yandy's number showed up. "That the old lady?" Jenny sipped her drink.

"Yeah," he answered grimly. Jenny gently pried the phone from his fingers then hit the power button to shut it off.

"You're with me tonight, baby." She then dropped it inside her glass.

The phone rang and Randy snatched it up.

"Hello." Rap music played in the background.

"It's Polo. I found the bitch, man. Hold on a minute . . ." Polo spoke to the woman sitting next to him. "Girl, don't you spill none of that shit on my leather seats. I'ma kick you and that drank's ass the fuck up outta here. Think I'm playing if—"

"Polo?"

"Yeah, I'm here. The bitch is staying at the Comfort Inn on Blue

Parkway. You want me to go in and knock that bitch's head off or what? You know I'm a killer." The woman next to him stared at him. "What? Yea, I said it, ho. You don't even know who you in the car with, do you?" Randy hung up on him. "Hello. Hello?" Polo said into the phone. "Damnit, bitch! You don' got me in trouble with the boss."

Randy's intentions were to go downstairs and have a drink with Morgen, but the news he had just received distracted him. He showered, shaved his head and face, then put on a blue pinstriped suit. He looked over his handsome reflection in the mirror to make sure he was up to par.

"Yeah," he said in regard to his looks. He adjusted the ring on his finger then shut the lights off as he walked out the door.

Randy drove his Porsche into the Comfort Inn parking lot and parked in front of Olivia's room. To be on the safe side, he took his nine millimeter along with him. Voices could be heard through the room door as Randy knocked but didn't receive an answer. After he glanced around and saw no one was watching, he kicked the door in. He didn't see anyone but the TV's volume was loud which explained where the voices came from. Randy entered with caution. First he checked the bathroom. Nothing. He lifted the mattress and a Polaroid picture was flat on its face. Randy picked it up and looked at it. He stared at a picture of Olivia laying in a hospital bed. Her lips were chapped and she looked to be about eighty pounds. Randy sighed before he stashed the photo inside his pocket then left.

## 18

It was two in the morning and Jenny still hadn't made it home. Randy had been calling her cell phone all night with no answer. Full of rage and anger, he threw the TV remote at his new parrot's birdcage. The huge bird flapped his wings desperately as he jumped from side to side. Randy called him Petey, short for "repeat."

"Fuckin' bitch!" Randy spat.

"Ock, bitch," the parrot mimicked.

"Shut up!"

"Shut up. Ock! Shut up." Randy paced the floor in his robe and slippers while drinking vodka straight out of the bottle. Fifteen minutes later he found himself calling the police stations and hospitals. None of them had heard of her. Vodka dribbled out of the corner of his mouth and he desperately needed something to smoke. Earlier that night he had gone out and bought three different kinds of weed. None of it had brought him to the level the stuff with Jenny brought him to. Randy picked up the phone again. To his surprise, somebody was already on the line.

"Hello."

"Hi, Randy. This is RiRi."

"RiRi?"

"Yes. I was just calling to see what you were doing all alone inside that big house."

"How did you know I was alone?" he asked suspiciously.

"Where's Jenny?"

"She left here hours ago with some rich guy," RiRi said truthfully. "Look, I get off soon. I'm coming over to keep you company." Randy didn't respond as he looked at his wedding ring. "Randy?"

"Yeah, bring some of that smoke with you. Bye." He let the phone fall to the floor. Shit was fucked up. He hadn't been married a month and already he was being cheated on. The bad thing about it was that he had really fallen for her. His heart was aching like it never had before. When RiRi showed up, she found herself looking at a pathetic figure. Randy's eyes were bloodshot, he only had on one house shoe, and he reeked of vodka. RiRi helped him to the bathroom where she bathed him then helped him into a fresh pair of underclothes before he stretched across the bed. Wearing one of Jenny's many sleep outfits, RiRi sat next to him on the bed and lit a joint. Randy sat up, anxiously awaiting his turn. She hit it a few good times before passing it to him. Randy took a good hit then another and another. Suddenly, he felt himself floating like a butterfly on cloud nine. He soared for about four minutes before he came in for a landing. A little while later he was feenin' for more. RiRi removed her panties and lay back on the bed.

"Eat me while I take a hit, baby," she said. Randy noticed that she was perspiring badly and her eyes were bulged. She was on her back, legs spread eagle, while he played Pac Man on her pussy lips.

After a minute, he came up for air. "Give me some." RiRi inhaled deeply then pressed her lips against his. The smoke traveled down his throat and filled his lungs. He had to back away after he began to choke. She sat up on her elbows with her head tilted back, enjoying her high. Randy's head cocked to the left as if he heard something. He jumped up.

"What's that?" he asked.

"I didn't hear anything."

His head cocked to the right. "There it is again."

RiRi sat up laughing. "There you go trippin'. You know what it is, baby? You're spooked. Paranoid. D-boys call it geekin'." She fell back laughing.

"Fuck you talking 'bout geekin', bitch? I'm not no fuckin'—" Randy glared down at the ashtray. He unraveled the butts but they were all burned up. "Get up!" he growled as he roughly grabbed her by her arm but she continued to laugh. "What the fuck is so funny, bitch?"

RiRi stopped laughing long enough to say, "You." Randy picked her up and threw her over his shoulder. She palmed his booty while he carried her through the living room. "C'mon, Randy, baby. Let's party, papi," she begged. "Don't throw me out."

Randy sat her on the front porch. "You too high, RiRi. Go the fuck home." He stood while she picked herself up. She slipped and almost busted her ass. Before RiRi had a chance to fully recover, he went back inside. Seconds later he returned with her purse, shoes, and clothes. He threw them at her then retreated inside. Rushing to the bathroom, he hit the light switch on his way to the sink. Gazing at his reflection in the mirror, he repeatedly told himself RiRi was only kidding until he started feening for more. Then he started believing her.

Jenny came home at 6:30 in the morning, carrying her shoes in her hand as she walked into the bedroom. Randy was wrapped in the covers snoring loudly. Her eyes were on him while she slipped out her dress and underwear. She went into the adjacent bathroom and turned on the shower. Standing in front of the mirror, she pulled back her hair and noticed a hickey on her neck. "He's a horny fat bastard," she said. Jenny peered down at the faucet and cut on the water. When her eyes shifted back to the mirror, Randy was standing behind her.

"Whoo!" she gasped.

"Why are you taking a shower?"

"Because I been fucking. Now would you excuse me so I can wash his scent off and go to bed?" she responded as she opened the shower door.

Randy took a step closer to her. "Would you mind repeating yourself? 'Cause I couldn't have heard you right."

"I said, I been fu—"

*Wack!*

Randy hit her so hard she fell backward into the tub under the hot shower water. She screamed as she squirmed to get up. He reached in, clutched her throat, and snatched her out. Terror was in her eyes.

"You got the wrong man, honey." He smacked her again while he held her throat. Blood ran from Jenny's lips as she kicked at his legs, trying desperately to get loose. Randy violently pushed her out the door and onto the floor. She grabbed her throat as she gasped for air. "I'ma teach yo' hot ass some respect," Randy warned. He took a leather belt out the closet. Jenny stood her naked body up and tried to break for the door, but he caught her by the waist then slammed her on the bed.

"Randy, please!" she begged.

"Don't hit me with—Owww—Owww! Ouch!" He viciously brought the strap down across her back, chest, and legs repeatedly.

Jenny scooted over the entire bed trying to dodge the heavy lashes. She fell over the side of the bed and scurried to the bathroom. By the time he got over there, she had kicked the door closed and locked it. He banged on the outside. "Go away!" Jenny screamed. Her flesh was on fire.

"You'd better lock yourself in, bitch," Randy yelled through the door. "You got me fucked up."

"I hate you!" Jenny screamed. "I'm leaving you."

Randy jiggled the knob. "Bitch, you lucky this door is too fuckin' expensive to break down." Jenny sat on the floor in front of the locked door with her knees up to her chest and cried. Randy dropped the belt then went and sat on the bed. He glanced at the roaches that were still in the ashtray.

He swore he actually heard little voices inside his head chanting, "Smoke me. Smoke me, damnit!" Against his better judgment, he picked up a roach and set fire to it. It was enough to take him to Lala Land and back. Before the sun rose, he had finished off every joint in the tray. The dope had him too geeked up to sleep. Instead, he paced every floor of the house, peeping out every window along the way. He could have sworn he saw the devil sitting on his front gate, swinging his legs while staring up at him. Randy ducked out the way. He wasn't sure what kind of sign that was. Had Lucifer himself come for him? Was he set to die tonight? When he looked again, the devil was no longer there. He was more than happy when it came time for him to leave for work. Jenny didn't come out of hiding until he left.

After Jenny left Morgen's hideaway, Morgen showered, changed clothes, and locked up. He hopped in his Lincoln and hit the highway. It was shocking to him that Yandy hadn't called to see where he was. Now he was left to wonder what she was doing that had her so busy. He smiled to himself as he fired up a cigarette. *Boy, that young, sweet Jenny was a great lay* he thought.

Man did he love the texture of a black woman's pussy. It was more a psychological thing with him because in reality they all felt the same. Some pussies were just tighter than others. Morgen picked up the phone and dialed ten numbers.

"Hello."

Yeah, this is Morgen. Can we meet?"

"I'm with my family."

"It's important."

The guy on the other line sighed. "Yeah, why not? Ahh . . . where?"

"How about the Waffle House on Main Street. I could use some breakfast."

"Okay." When Morgen arrived at the restaurant, he ordered breakfast and a paper. He was reading the *Money* section when he saw his associate's car pull into the parking lot. He folded his paper and sipped on the hot coffee as the guy walked through the door. Mrs. Kastening, the manager, smiled at him.

"Hi," she said with a smile. "How's things out in the field?"

Detective Madison inhaled. "Well, Janice, they don't make criminals like they used to." He peered at Morgen. "Yep, these days, there's a rat amongst every crew." She laughed as she walked away. Madison ordered a large coffee before he joined Morgen at his table. He stared into Morgen's eyes while smacking his gum. "Mornin'." Morgen nodded. Madison looked out the window. "Look, Morgen, I know that you and this fellow, Randy, were in on the bank robberies. You were his inside connection. I know that because now you guys are suddenly in business together, parading around town like the best of friends."

"All you know is what I tell you."

Madison shrugged. "Maybe so, Morgen, but I'm not a dummy either." He accepted his cup of coffee from the waitress and tasted it. "Coffee's a little strong this morning. So what's up? You wanted to see me, you rat motherfucker? What's so important you dragged me out of the house before my shift starts?"

Morgen smirked. "You asshole. You used to work for me, making sure the law stayed off my ass. Now that you got a promotion and we swap a little information here and there I'm a rat motherfucker?"

"Sure you are, Morgen," he stated calmly. "You get your hands dirty right along with an accomplice to obtain businesses. Then when business reaches its max you decide to take it all by yourself, ratting out your business partners to the cops." He leaned in close. "Tell me something, do you take care of them while they're on the inside?"

Morgen looked him in the eyes. "I only betray them after they betray me."

"So you say." They stared at each other.

"What do you want from me?"

"I want Randy gone."

"How? If we take him in for these robberies, we'd have to take you. I'm covering the fact those security tapes of yours did not show clear pictures of the suspects so give me something else."

Morgen rubbed his chin. "I'll come up with something."

"Well don't take long. I want this guy bad. It'll make me look good.

If you don't come up with something quick, then I'll just have to take both of you down." He stood and picked a piece of sausage off Morgen's plate, and Morgen glared at him.

"You seem to have forgotten who helped pay the mortgage on your house."

"I forgot that after I made the last payment five years ago. And not one cent of that money can be traced. Look, we go way back, Morgen, but I got a job to do." He took two steps, stopped, and turned around. "By the way, I wanna pay my wife's car off too . . . this month. You think you can help me?"

"After I'm satisfied, you'll get taken care of."

"Fair enough."

Randy returned home around eight o'clock that night, way earlier than usual. When he walked into the house, he smelled the seasoned aroma of good food cooking. The house was spotless, the table in the dining room was set for one, and there were candles lit. Jenny came jogging out of the kitchen with an apron on. She wore a big smile on her face when she approached him. First there was a kiss then she removed his jacket and pulled out the chair for him.

"Have a seat and kick off your shoes. Dinner will be ready in a minute." Randy saw that she wore plenty of makeup, possibly to shield the bruises on her face.

"Cut the shit, Jenny. What's up?" Randy asked suspiciously.

She massaged his shoulders. "It's just my way of saying I'm sorry. I love you, daddy. I'm supposed to be punished after I've been bad. I just hope that you find it in your heart to forgive me." She watched as he stood and planted a kiss on her lips. She broke the embrace. "Relax yourself, Randy. Let me do all the work." She left and returned with a sirloin and baked potatoes. While he ate she massaged his feet. After he finished, she washed him up like she was his servant then took off her clothes and rested in his arms. He wrapped his arms around her.

"Mm, this feels good, daddy," Jenny said softly. Her eyes were closed. "I love being in your arms."

"I'm sorry for hitting you." He kissed her head but she laughed it off.

"I deserved it. I don't mind a good ass whoopin' when I've been bad. You see how that belt put me in my place, don't you?"

Randy smiled. "I wasn't gonna say nothing but I did notice a change in your attitude."

"Daddy?"

"Yeah?"

"I wanna go shopping at the Lennox Mall in Atlanta this weekend, maybe kick it at a club or two. I've never been there." Randy circled her nipple with his finger.

"Anything else?"

"Yes." She turned around and kissed his chest. "I love you, daddy."

"You too."

"I want you to spoil me like a child. Make me feel good. I promise I'ma make you proud."

That weekend Randy and Jenny, along with Polo and his broad, flew down to Atlanta on a chartered flight. The first attraction they visited was Zoo Atlanta. They enjoyed a nice walk around the zoo, looking at the animals while sharing a drink. That afternoon Randy took Jenny to buy up the mall and the night ended with dinner at Spondivits where they dined on lobster and shrimp. By the end of the night, they were so exhausted they spent the night cuddled in their hotel room watching movies. Saturday they went to Six Flags. Randy tried his best to win Jenny a stuffed toy but luck wasn't on his side that day. He ended up having to buy her one. Though it wasn't the same as winning one, Jenny appreciated the effort. Age must have taken a toll on him because the roller coasters were getting the best of him. He had thrown up twice. On the second go-round, Jenny had to ride with a young man she met at the park. Randy waited at the gate while eating a funnel cake.

That night they dressed for the club and before they left Randy surprised her with the platinum and diamond bracelet set he purchased earlier and had delivered. They all rode to the club in a chauffeured stretch Navigator. The line to get into the club was about a mile long, but Randy thought too highly of himself to wait in line so he escorted Jenny to the front. It took only a moment and a hundred dollars to persuade the doorman to let them inside ahead of every-body else. Inside the club, they got their drink and their dance on. Jenny was a bit too fast for the old dog at first but after his second wind kicked in he was shaking a tail feather.

Randy left Jenny to go to the restroom and while he was away the guy Jenny met at Six Flags spotted her sitting alone. She was bobbing her head, looking at the dancers on the floor. The guy ordered himself a drink from the bar and strutted over to her table. He was already sitting before Jenny even noticed him.

Jenny smiled. "Hi, Tracy." She pushed her hair out of her face.

"Hey. What are you doing here alone, girl? What happened to your old man?"

"Umm," she glanced around the room, "he's in the restroom."

"If he's in there doin' the number two, then we have time for one dance."

"Okay." Tracy swallowed a big gulp of his drink before he led her out on the floor. Jenny turned her back to him, dancing slowly and seductively as she grinded her ass against his crotch. He was smooth with it as his hands held onto her small waist while their hips swayed from left to right to the rhythm of the beat. His thin fingers felt like tickling feathers as they traveled up and down her body.

"Let's get outta here," Tracy whispered in her ear.

Jenny peered in the direction of the restroom but she didn't see Randy. "Let me grab my purse." Moments later Randy came out of the restroom wiping his hands on a paper towel. He spoke to several young ladies on his way back to his table. Jenny's drink and an odd drink were resting on the table when he arrived but his wife was nowhere to be found. He scanned the room as the waitress started picking up the glasses.

"You seen the lady I came in with?" Randy inquired.

"Um hm," she answered. "She left a minute ago with Tracy."

"Tracy?" Randy mistakenly took the name for a female's.

"Um hm," she confirmed and Randy raced for the exit.

Polo was sitting at the table with his girl when he saw Randy take off. He immediately rose from his seat. "Be right back, baby." Randy reached the front of the club and looked around the entire lot for any sign of his wife, as girls coming and going hissed and gawked at him. Polo came behind him. "What's going on, man?"

"This bitch don'—" He spotted Jenny getting into the passenger side of a Honda Accord. "Follow me." Tracy slipped his tongue inside Jenny's mouth as he eased his hand under her skirt. She let the seat back so he could get a good feel and she giggled while Tracy freaked her. Her eyes popped open when she heard the car door snatch open. Polo reached in and snatched Tracy out the car.

"Hey!" Tracy hollered. "Ahh!" he grunted as Polo hit him in the stomach. Tracy fell to the ground and Randy kicked him repeatedly until blood drained from his mouth.

"Didn't OJ teach you bitches about cheating on a rich nigga with a broke nigga?" Polo asked Jenny. Randy pulled her out the car by her neck, forcing her to look at Tracy.

"Look at 'em!" Randy demanded. "Next time I catch you fuckin' around with one of these young niggas, that's gonna happen to you. Ya hear me, bitch?" A large crowd started to gather. "C'mon." He tightly held her arm while he spoke to Polo. "Take care of this and catch a cab back to the hotel."

"Okay." Randy literally dragged Jenny to the Navigator and shoved her inside. He got in and slammed the door. "What the fuck is wrong with you?" he asked angrily as the car began to move. "Every time I—"

"You had no right to do what you did!" Jenny yelled. "I'm a grown goddamn woman and if I want to fuck around I'ma fuck a—" Randy punched her in the eye, causing her head to slam into the window. She held her hand up to her eye while purring sounds escaped her lips. "Ouch! You pussy!" she shouted as the truck slowly turned the corner. "Don't put your fuckin' hands on me again." She opened the door of the moving vehicle, but Randy reached around her and slammed it shut. "Driver, let me out!" she hollered.

"I can't do that. Girl, you might get lost down here."

"I'd rather be lost in Atlanta than dead in the back of this truck." While she screamed at the driver, she reached into her purse and fished out her pocketknife. Randy heard the clicking sound of the knife opening a second too late.

"Owww!" he screamed when he felt the knife entering his right arm.

"Get out!" Jenny screamed, twisting the knife to dig deeper. Randy fumbled for the door handle until he found it and pulled it. The light came on when the door opened so the driver instantly pulled over on Peachtree. An oncoming car hit its brakes when Randy fell out the truck and onto the street holding his arm. Jenny got out and stood over him, tightly clutching the knife in her hand. Carefully, Randy removed his jacket and shirt. It was only a small wound but he almost fainted when he saw the fat meat hanging out of it.

"Bitch, you tried to kill me!" he shouted. "I swear to God, I'ma fuck you up." A black BMW pulled over and the driver stepped out to make sure they were alright. Southern hospitality. Jenny ran over to him and persuaded him to take her away from the scene. The limo driver helped Randy up. He spat on the window of the BMW as it sped past. "Don't bring yo' ass back!" he yelled. "Bitch ruined my fuckin' jacket."

Back at the hotel, Randy sat out on the balcony lusting for Jenny and something to smoke besides cigarettes. He didn't want to admit it but he was beginning to feel like he had taken on a habit he didn't need. Just to be sure, he caught a cab down to the projects and copped a quarter bag of green and a fifty-dollar piece of crack. As instructed by the junkie cabby, he copped a used glass pipe for fifty dollars. Back inside the hotel room he laced three joints with sprinkles of crack then stripped naked and climbed into a tub of hot water.

*Randy, what the fuck are you about to do?* he heard himself say inside his head. *Don't do it, man.* He fired up one of the joints and locked the smoke inside his lungs for a long as he could then released a thick white cloud of smoke into the air. "Goddamn," he said as a smile grew on his face. He had found it. The high he was looking for other than Jenny. And it was indeed crack cocaine. If someone would have told him sixteen years ago he would be a crackhead, he would have shot them dead. An hour later, all three of the joints were gone and so was the high.

The bath water had grown cold and he was ready to quit, but the monkey dancing on his back wasn't finished just yet. He was still craving that high. His head rolled to the right and his eyes locked on the crack pipe sitting next to the tub. Licking his dry lips, he reached for the glass. His hand cupped it but he hesitated for a second to think about what he was doing. He knew once he turned down that road there was a great chance he would never return. Ever.

"I'm stronger than that," he told himself. "One last time. I promise I won't get hooked." Randy picked up the glass, stuffed it with crack, struck a match and sealed their union. The drug hit him so hard his heart nearly exploded. When the pipe dropped to the floor, his head fell backward.

*Thump! Thump!*

"What's that?" He jumped out of the tub when he thought he heard the hotel door opening. He sprung out of the bathroom. From under the mattress, he pulled out his nine millimeter and drew it but no one was there.

*Thump! Thump!*

Randy's heart also began to thump while his eyes darted around the room. The thumping grew louder.

*Thump! Thump!*

Randy whirled around, shot the couch twice, and ran out the door butt naked. Later he chartered a plane back home without Jenny, Polo or his girl.

The woman was the first to climb over the wall behind Randy's house then the man followed her lead. The two vicious Dobermans came running from the front of the house and their barking grew louder as they came near.

*Roof! Roof!*

The two thieves stood still. For a moment, it seemed like the dogs were going to attack them until the woman pulled up her mask. The dogs stopped immediately. She held out her hand so they could smell her scent. While she occupied them, the man walked ahead. He found the circuit box on the side of the house and the tiny flashlight showed him what he needed to see. He clipped the hotwire that powered the alarm then whistled for the woman to come on. The woman removed a small crowbar from the black leather bag she carried and he used it to pop the screen door before she went to work on the deadbolt. A minute later they walked inside.

Quickly but quietly, they moved through the house on their way to his office. Behind his desk was a small file cabinet secured by a combination lock. She opened her bag again and her partner removed a small torch to set fire to it then went to work. With the skill of a trained thief, he cut a near perfect circle around the lock. When it fell off, the girl stuck a screwdriver through the hole and turned until she heard a click. The man opened the drawer, searching until he found what they were looking for. When he found it, they left back the way they came.

# 19

Randy sat around the conference table surrounded by members of the gaming commission, investment bankers, the mayor, and Morgen. His eyes were bloodshot red and he appeared to have been up for days. The suit that he sat slumped in was not as crisp as usual and his hands fidgeted. Morgen shot daggers across the room at him. Not because they had gotten into it the last time they spoke but because Jenny had talked a bunch of bullshit in his ear. She had told Morgen a bunch of dirty things about Randy, and as they were in the meeting, Jenny was asleep in one of Morgen's apartments. Randy didn't hear one word that was spoken. He was too busy trying to figure out who would break into his home and steal copies of the black book.

It could have been some of Fredrick's people but the fact that the intruders went right to the cabinet said it was an inside job. That could have been Spud or Jenny. Or maybe they were in it together? But at what gain? Maybe they were planning to sell it back to Fredrick. Whatever the case, Fredrick was going to have to die. Randy couldn't take the chance of his name getting mixed up in that. There was too much at stake.

Before the meeting was adjourned, Randy stood and announced

he wanted to say something. "Ah, I want to," he stopped to clear this throat. "I think it would be a good idea if we invest in and build a treatment center for drug addicts as well as battered women. Uh, not only would it be good for business, but publicity as well for you, Mr. Mayor." They all nodded in agreement.

"Good idea, Mr. Harris," the mayor complimented. "I nominate that to be the next thing on our agenda. All in favor?"

"Aye," everyone loudly uttered as Randy nodded and took a seat.

"Ladies and gentlemen, this meeting is adjourned," the chairman announced.

"Uh, excuse me," Morgen said. "If you gentlemen would for a minute, please listen to what I have to say." He stood and placed one hand in his pocket. "I vote we remove Randy Harris from the board."

"Why?" the chairman asked.

"Well, first because he's an ex-felon." Everybody focused their attention on Randy after they heard the word "ex-felon" and Randy's chin dropped. "Secondly," Morgen continued. "he's being investigated for a string of robberies. And last, I have good reason to believe he's a drug addict and he should be ordered to submit a urine sample to be tested for narcotics." Randy fought hard to remain in control of himself. He could not believe what Morgen had done to him, putting his business on the table like that. Morgen knew it wouldn't do Randy any good to involve him in the bank robbery conspiracy because his tracks were covered and he had the law backing him. The board faced Randy.

The chairman asked, "Mr. Harris? What do you have to say about these accusations?"

Randy ran his hand over his face. "Well, Mr. Chairman, I don't know where Mr. Morgen gets his information but I can assure you it's false."

The mayor addressed the chairman. "I'll look into it. You have my word on that. And Randy, if these accusations are confirmed, consider yourself fired, and you will be brought up on charges."

"I understand, Mr. Mayor."

"Randy, you will remain manager of this casino until the matter is resolved. After the New Year, however, you'll be placed on paid leave until the conclusion of a thorough investigation. Is that clear, Mr. Harris?" the chairman stated and Randy nodded.

"Perfectly."

"Alright. Once again, this meeting is adjourned." All the men stood, gathered their things, and whispered to the person next to them as they filed out the room. Randy remained seated as Morgen stood and looked out the window. They waited until everybody left.

"You shouldn't have disrespected me in your office that night, Randy. On top of that, you stood me up at the bar."

Randy stood slowly. "You wanna end my career over some bullshit like that? A fuckin' argument?"

"It may have been just an argument to you, Randy!" Morgen yelled. "But to me, it was about respect. Hell, I'm the goddamn reason you're living the way you're living, boy. Then you go and talk to me like some fuckin' nigger? Fuck you! Your tough ass is going down!"

Randy grabbed Morgen by his throat and slammed him on the table. He snatched the telephone cord out of the wall and wrapped it tightly around his neck. Morgen's face and neck turned red as a tomato as he kicked and squirmed under the pressure. After a few seconds, Randy released him. While Randy walked away, Morgen stood gagging and holding his throat.

"You're a dead motherfucker! You don't have to worry about getting removed," he threatened. "I'm taking you out. You think that monkey's on your goddamn back? I'm gonna be up your ass like a shitty thong." Randy slammed the door behind him, breaking the glass window.

Randy jumped into his Porsche and got on the phone.

"Hello."

"Polo, I need you to holla at Fredrick for me."

"Holla at him for what?"

"No, I mean *holla at him*. See if he was involved in what happened to my house the other night. I want him silenced. I don't need my name mixed up in no bullshit, especially right now. And I'm thinking ... never mind."

"A'ight, I'll get on it."

"Thanks." He was thinking Jenny and Morgen might somehow be involved with each other. They had to be. How else could Morgen be so sure of his drug usage? Jenny wasn't home when Randy arrived so he put on some sweats and a T-shirt to get comfortable. Something had to be done. By tomorrow, the mayor would know his whole background by placing one phone call and that would be the end of Randy Harris. He'd have three million dollars' worth of the hotel's stock but Randy couldn't let it end like that. Not just yet.

After all the money he had been spending on his house, cars, wedding, jewelry, and donations, his cash level wasn't that high. His credit was long but that would go with his job. He had to think of something to keep his money rolling.

As stressed as he was, Randy wondered how he could think at all. He needed something to help calm his nerves. Something neither the weed or drink could handle. He needed that almighty feeling that could only be obtained by crack.

"This'll be my last time," he promised himself as he reached for his car keys. It was a little after one in the morning as he drove down to his old neighborhood. The corner hustlers were probably in for the night but it was worth a try. A young man about nineteen was standing on the corner of 57th Street along with a crackhead runner. He saw the Porsche coming down the block and knew only two types of people drove a car like that through the hood—a baller or some rich white man looking to get high.

"See who that is, Smiley," he ordered the crackhead. "Ask him do he want to rent out his car."

"Okay." Smiley walked up to the Porsche when it pulled over, and Randy let the window down.

"Anybody holdin'?" He couldn't believe what he had just said. Smiley peered at his face really good.

"You the police?"

"C'mon, man. I'm driving a fuckin' Porsche. Now what's up? I'm not trying to get busted here."

"What you tryna get?"

"Gimme something for a hundred."

"Hold on." Smiley left to talk to the hustler. While he was doing that, Randy searched his pockets for his wallet and realized he had left it in his suit jacket. *Damn!* He wouldn't be able to get credit here and the monkey was calling him. Randy refused to leave empty handed. He was too good of a thief. What he couldn't buy, he stole but he didn't have his gun either. Smiley walked back over to the car clutching a chunk of crack in his hands.

"What you got?" Randy inquired nervously.

"Where's the money?" Randy smiled. "C'mon, man, I'm rich. I'm not tryna fuck you. Let me see what I'm paying for." Smiley stuck the dope in the window, and Randy hungrily eyed it as it sat in Smiley's hand. With the quickness of a striking snake, Randy hit Smiley's hand, forcing the dope to fall in the car before he hit the gas. Randy almost reached the corner when he heard gunshots.

*Boc! Boc! Boc!*

One of the bullets went through his back window but he didn't let off the gas. He made it all the way out to a nearby dead-end street where he parked at a vacant house. Anxiously, he dug the piece out from between the door and seat then took the pipe out his pocket. After he loaded a piece onto it, he took a blast. For two hours, he sat in the car getting spooked until half of the chunk was gone. Around 3:30 that morning he drove off. When he peered in his rearview mirror, he thought he saw the devil sitting in his backseat.

"Ahhh!" he screamed, opening his door. He leapt out and rolled across the street. Cars came to a screeching halt, trying to prevent collisions. The Porsche veered off the road and jumped the curb but stopped when a light pole. Randy was unconscious when the ambulance arrived to pick him up but he woke up alone in a hospital room. A quick check of his fingers, toes, and a turn of his neck told him he was all right. He only suffered from a few scratches and bruises and a terrible headache. Other than that, he seemed to be fine. The shocking thing was there weren't any newspaper representatives trying to get a story. Randy picked up the phone and dialed Yandy's number. He was feeling lonely and needed someone to reach out to. The phone only rang once before the voicemail picked up.

Patiently, he waited for the recording to end before he started speaking. "Yandy, this is Randy."

Yandy pulled her tongue out of Spud's mouth and looked over at the phone as Spud was on top of her, deep in her crevice. She reached for it but Spud grabbed her arm.

"Wait, I wanna hear this."

"I'm sorry for the way I treated you," Randy continued. "Man, I feel so alone and . . . and I wish I had my friend to talk to."

Spud chuckled. "Listen to him. He's begging. His big head has gotten too heavy for him to hold up." "Yandy?" Spud reached over and hung up the phone then placed himself back inside of her and went back to humping. Yandy held onto his back, even moaned while he handled his business. Physically, she was there but her mind was on Randy. She thought of how they had violated him by robbing his house. Fredrick had contacted her by phone and offered her a million dollars for his black book. After consulting with Spud who knew about it and where the copies were, she offered to sell Fredrick the copies. It was the best she could do. Fredrick agreed to purchase the copied version for seven hundred and fifty thousand, but she didn't leak to Fredrick where she obtained the copies. She wouldn't stoop that low.

Spud sensed Randy was on her mind and not the dick he was giving her so he dug in deep, hitting bottom. Yandy let out an uncontrollable howl that could have very well awakened the neighbors. Suddenly, she cleared Randy from her thoughts and focused on the meat that filled her insides. Right now, she would focus on reaching an orgasm. Randy would come after.

Randy slowly placed the phone down then laid back in bed as fatigue settled in on him. Just as his eyes fluttered shut someone busted into the room and his eyes popped open.

"Oh, my God!" Jenny said. "Baby, what happened?" She sat down on the bed next to him.

"Had an accident."

"The doctor said you suffered a mild concussion. They also said you're lucky you weren't killed."

"Where you been?" Randy shot her a cold look and she looked away.

"I needed to be alone for a minute, you know?" She massaged her hands. "After I stabbed you, I got scared."

"Scared of what?"

"Of everything. Of being tied down, of losing my youth." She stood and started fiddling with things. "I wasn't sure if I wanted to be married."

"Yeah, well I'm not so sure now either."

"What is that supposed to mean?"

"You know exactly what I'm saying. Tell me something . . . how does Morgen know so much about my drug habit?"

"Morgen?" she said in a low voice as if she couldn't remember who he was. "I . . . I . . . don't know—"

"Bitch, don't lie to me now."

"Baby, don't let this bullshit get your blood pressure up." Her tone was serious. " I said I don't know so let's leave it at that. I have no reason to lie to you." She kneeled next to the bed and cupped his face in her hands. "I realize I'm wrong for treating you like I do, but I love you and wouldn't betray you." She suddenly stopped. "Drug habit?"

"Yes, drug habit. Or don't you know nothing about that?" Jenny stared at her feet, and Randy bit his bottom lip. "I'm a crackhead now. All because I'm in love, drunk, and sprung off young pussy."

"I'm an addict too, Randy," she stated softly. "I guess I wanted us both to experience the same thing. I thought that maybe . . . just maybe you and I could kick this thing. I don't know 'bout you but I can't do it alone." She got down on her knees and held his hand. "Please, let's start over. I love you."

That was all game coming from her lips and Randy knew it, but it worked. He peered at her sneaky looking pretty face and wanted so bad to throw her out but something inside of him wanted to help her. If he could save her by helping her get on the right track, then it would help improve their relationship. "We don't need no doctors," Jenny said. "Together, with our love alone, we can kick the habit. That's why I done it. That was the only for sure way I could get help." The mayor barged into the room unannounced. He stopped at the foot of Randy's bed with his hands on his hips and glared at him. Randy could read his body language.

"Jenny, could you excuse us for a moment?" Randy said.

"Sure." Jenny kissed him on his cheek then whispered, "Am I forgiven?" Randy painfully nodded his head and she made her exit.

The mayor glanced over his shoulder until Jenny was gone then sighed heavily.

"The doctors did some blood work on you. Do you know what they found?"

Randy lowered his head. "Cocaine."

"Cocaine. Can you imagine how disappointed I was when I found that out?" Randy didn't respond. "You can thank me that the reporters aren't in here jamming microphones up your sorry ass."

"Thank you," Randy responded humbly. "I am grateful."

"You're gonna be more than grateful. See, politics are exactly like you see on TV and everything you've ever heard. It's dirty, and it costs to play in our game."

Randy poured himself a cup of water and drank it all. "How much?"

"Twenty-five thousand, cash. To be paid immediately." The mayor walked to the door and turned around. "And if you want that background of yours to disappear before the investigation starts, it's gonna cost you another twenty-five grand. We never had this conversation."

"I'll have," Randy coughed, "Polo get you the money by tomorrow evening."

"I don't trust drug addicts but just this one time I'ma take a chance." The mayor left.

"You ain't got no fuckin' choice, you fuckin' cocksucker," Randy said to himself.

## 20

S pud and Big Boi had been tailing the armored truck all day and it made several stops before it arrived at the hotel. The security guards walked into the hotel at approximately 7:47 p.m. and walked out ten minutes later carrying black bags.

"We're gonna take 'em at the grocery store," Spud said to Big Boi as the two were parked a little ways behind the truck. They had all the information they needed and a plan to enter and exit the hotel with the money. If things went the way they planned, the whole thing would go smoothly. Big Boi took several photographs of the guards. "Get a shot of the gun holes on the truck," Spud suggested.

Big Boi snapped a few more shots. "Got 'em." He peered over at Spud. "Don't it feel weird plotting to rob Randy?"

Spud placed a cigarette between his lips. "Of course not. The man snaked us so it's only right." He put the car in drive. "Besides, a lot of that money goes to taxes, investors, and so forth. So, in reality, we're robbing the goddamn state. It's all insured anyway. He'd be proud of us knowing we were able to plan and pull off a heist like this one." Spud drove away.

"Assuming we pull it off," Big Boi whispered to himself.

Meanwhile, Yandy was walking along the plaza. She had on a flashy dress, a full-length mink coat, and dark shades. She suddenly stopped to look inside the window of a clothing store but she wasn't admiring the clothing. Yandy was looking at the reflection of the man across the street staring at her. Madison moved swiftly though the crowd of Christmas shoppers trying to catch up to Detective Law who was standing in front of a building looking across the street at Yandy. She dipped inside the store for a little while.

"What's happening?" Madison asked, finally catching up.

"Nothing yet, browsing through a few store windows."

Madison scanned the area with his eyes. "She's up to something. You can believe that." Suddenly, Yandy burst out the store's door, moving at a fast pace. "Let's go," Madison said. Yandy walked west to the corner, made a right, then another right until she came upon a jewelry store. After staring up at the sign for a minute, she walked in. Madison and Law stopped running and tried to catch their breath. "How did you get onto her?" Madison asked.

"An informant sent me a message saying something about a robbery on the plaza. I was hoping it might be them so I came down here and drove around for a little while, you know? Just to see what's down here worth robbing. That's when I spotted her."

Madison looked at the jewelry store then peered around the semi secluded area on the plaza. That's when it hit him. "This is the place."

"What place?"

"Where it's all gonna go down. They'll take down the jewelry store then we'll take them down." Law could see Yandy inside the store chatting with the clerk. She had a platinum ring in her hand with a huge diamond on it.

"I think you're right, Madison."

"Of course, I'm right." A gray Cadillac pulled in front of the store, and Yandy casually walked out the store with nothing in her hands as she climbed into the backseat. The car bolted away and Madison walked into the middle of the street as the car made a sharp right before it disappeared. "Get on the phone and get me an around the clock surveillance team set up in this area. Not only are they watching the store but this entire perimeter." He smacked his gum. "I'ma enjoy taking that slick bitch down."

"What about Randy?"

"He's in it with 'em. Though he might not physically take part in the heist, you bet the hair on your ass he's in on it. I have good faith we'll have enough to nail his ass too."

"They take the bait?" Spud asked over his shoulder.

Yandy took out her cigarettes and fired one up before she answered. "We'll know later, won't we?"

Big Boi turned around, peering over the seat at Yandy. His eyes traveled down her coat and his stare landed on her cleavage. "You know, you have some really big tits, Yandy."

"You're not snorting nothing off them, Big Boi, but thanks for the compliment."

Big Boi frowned as he turned back around. *She ended that before it even got started but that's okay* he thought. *I know she wants to fuck me. I saw how—*

"C'mere, Big Boi," Spud blurted, interrupting him.

"Huh?"

"C'mere for a second." Big Boi leaned toward him.

*Smack!*

"Hey!" Big Boi held his jaw. "What the hell—"

"You talk too fuckin' much. Now sit yo' ass back and shut the fuck up!" While they were arguing, Yandy sat back and began daydreaming about Randy. He was supposed to be her soul mate, yet she wasn't who he wanted. When he called and left that message, she saved it and replayed it twenty times. It only proved she still had feelings for him. She returned the call that night after Spud left but there was no answer. What kind of games were he playing? Her feelings were all mixed up about what she should do. He had dogged her for a younger woman. That was understandable because that was just life but when he called the other night Yandy took it as a cry for help. His new young bride wasn't all she was cracked up to be. Yandy made up her mind. The cat was not going to keep chasing the dog. If he called her before the new ear, then she would try to call off the heist. If he didn't, things would go as planned. And she would have no remorse.

Randy stood behind his office desk turning the dial on his safe. When it opened, he took out fifty thousand and placed it on his desk. He heard the toilet in his restroom flush and Polo came out, buttoning his pants. He nodded toward the money on the desk.

"Is that it?"

"Yes. Run it over to the mayor's office. Pull around back and he'll have someone come out and get it." He took a seat as Polo put the money in a bag.

"Be back in a few."

"Any word on Fredrick?"

"Man, I been lookin' all over for that clown but I can't find him. Don't worry, I will."

"Good. The sooner the better." Once Randy was alone he started going over some paperwork until the monkey called him again. He tried to ignore it and concentrate on what he was doing. Before long, he started scratching his arms and his body started twitching. "No," he told himself but the monkey wouldn't let up. Randy knew he would not survive the hour without a hit so he devised a plan. Each time he would take a smaller hit until he weaned himself off the narcotic. It wouldn't work because deep down he loved the high. He called downstairs and had RiRi sent up. She arrived minutes later looking nervous.

"Am I fired?" Her hands fidgeted.

"Not yet," he replied. "You got any stuff on you? I know you do so cut the bullshit." RiRi put her purse on the desk then pulled one of the chairs up to it. She emptied out a pipe, lighter, and a plastic bag.

"Let's go in the bathroom," she suggested.

"Let's do some here first. I'm achin' like a muthafucka." Randy waited anxiously for her to break the rock down and load the pipe. She took the first blast then passed it to him. The longer he hit it, the larger his eyes swelled. It took a while for the high to kick in because the batch wasn't as good as usual. When it finally did kick in, he became instantly spooked. His head slowly turned in RiRi's direction. "Who are you? How did you get onto me?"

RiRi regarded him like he was crazy. "What? C'mon, don't start wiggin' out on me. You're gonna blow my high."

"Who sent you?" Randy leapt from his seat and slapped her in the face. He clutched her shoulders and violently shook her. "Who sent you?"

RiRi started crying as blood dripped from her lip. "No one."

"Get the fuck outta here!" He threw her to the floor. "Get!"

"My purse!" Randy flung it at her as she stumbled out. He walked back to the desk and just as he was about to take another blast someone knocked at the door. "Who is it?" He pulled on the pipe.

"Your wife."

He snatched open the desk drawer and scraped everything into it. *Bitch ain't gettin' none of this* he thought. "Come in."

Jenny strutted in wearing her work uniform; boy shorts, a sports bra, and knee-high boots. "Hi, husband." She seemed cheerful. He allowed her a peck on the cheek before he hurried to the bathroom. He brushed and rinsed away the awful crack smell from his breath. Jenny beat on the door. "Baby." Randy opened it and she jumped into his arms, kissing his cheeks. He winced from the pain in his aching bones. He still hadn't fully recovered from the accident. They fell onto the couch, kissing. "I love you, daddy," Jenny said with a smile. His high had vanished as he caressed her cheek. "You feel awfully thin. What have you been eating?" she inquired. Randy thought about her question. He hadn't really eaten since they were in Atlanta because the dope had stripped him of his appetite.

"I think it's the shit," he admitted. "I haven't been hungry since I tried the glass."

"I'm sorry." She looked at him sincerely. "Baby, after the new year, I'ma sign us up for rehab, okay?"

Randy rubbed his head. The thought of living in a rehab center didn't sit well with him. It was for bums and crackheads. *Wait a minute . . . I am a crackhead.*

"On New Year's Eve, while the fight is going on, let's get a suite and enjoy each other's company. What do you say?"

He nudged his nose against hers. "Okay. Sounds fun." He stared into her pretty eyes and almost lost his breath. Looking at her, he knew what it was about her that had his nose wide open. Her youth. Chasing and fighting with Jenny made him feel young again, like he was living out the life he had lost behind bars. Yandy made him feel like the middle-aged man he was, but that wasn't who he wanted to be. That was why he so easily took on the drug habit. It took him away for a moment, not caring if he was old. Crack took away every aching pain in his body and lifted his spirits as high as the heavens. "You were right, you know that?" Randy admitted.

"About what?"

"You're in control. You've caught me. I can't control you like I can't control it. Ever since you came in my life it has changed dramatically . . . Really for the worse, but at the same time, for the better."

"Well." Jenny looked down at her lap. "I'ma do my best to make it all for the better this time around."

"How?" he inquired.

"By being a good wife, as well as your friend. Okay?" Randy nodded.

Polo got off at the downtown exit and drove to City Hall. He pulled in front looking for the mayor's aide. A tall white man wearing a black trench coat and dark shades walked down the steps and Polo let him in.

"Pull away from here," the man instructed and Polo became angry.

"Look, man, I thought you were supposed to grab the money and go?"

"There's been a change of plans. Turn left at the corner." Polo made the left then another left and drove until the man told him to pull into an alley behind a building.

"Man, where the fuck is you taking me? I got a bitch waiting on me back at the hotel." He looked at his phone to see if he had any missed calls.

"Don't worry about it," the man said. "You're not gonna make your appointment."

"What—"

"Stop the fuckin' car!" he ordered and pulled a gun. Polo stopped and put the car in park. He heard the back door open and someone got in but didn't take his eyes off the man who held him at gunpoint. The first chance he got he had to make a move. The man in the front seat looked toward the back and said, "When—"

In one swift motion, Polo grabbed the gun and pushed it toward the ceiling. Two shots went through the roof. While he was tussling with the man in the front seat, the second man wrapped a piece of wire around Polo's neck, pulling him backward.

"Urggh!" Polo lost his wind but didn't give up as his hands remained on the gun. Polo lifted his leg and knocked the gear out of park with his knee then hit the gas.

"Nooo!" The car crashed into the building. The front airbags deployed and struck Polo and the front seat passenger in the face. The man in the back seat jerked forward and collided hard with the headrest, causing him to release the wire. With one hand still on the passenger's gun, Polo used his other to slide his own out his waist. Though the airbag was in the way, it wouldn't stop the bullet from getting to its target.

*Boc! Boc!*

Blood squirted out the man's chest all over the front seat. The interior light came on when the back door opened. Polo pointed the gun over the seat at the man's already bloody face.

"Where the fuck you think you goin'?"

"I . . . I . . ."

"I tried to tell them niggas I was a coldblooded killer." The man tried to flee but Polo quickly ended his escape.

*Boc! Boc! Boc!*

His head fell backward as his eyes stared at the ceiling while blood seeped from the three holes across his forehead.

Yandy pulled into the lot of the Comfort Inn Hotel off the highway. She touched up her makeup in the mirror then went to knock on the door. Detective Law answered, wearing his work shirt, boxers, and black socks. She kissed him on the lips as she kicked the door closed.

"Mm, did they buy it, baby?" she asked.

"Yep. They think y'all are plotting to rob the jewelry store."

"Good." She kissed him again. "You did good, baby." After the bank robberies occurred, Law found Yandy's file and decided to use her to get paid. He started by dropping notes in her mailbox until they finally met up at The Cheesecake Factory. Law showed her pictures of his son, Andrew, and explained he needed a hundred and twenty-five thousand for an operation that his insurance refused to cover. He had been turned down after applying for several loans and he was down to his last option. Yandy agreed to get in cahoots with him. To be sure it wasn't a trap, she used her pussy as a weapon to open his nose. Once she got him hooked, she gave him his first assignment to keep the cops off their tail while they took down the casino. So far, he had done a good job.

"So, when do I get my money?" he asked eagerly. "Andrew is running out of time."

Yandy fiddled with her skirt. "Like I told you, half now," it fell to the floor, "half later."

## 21

T he next morning Randy sat at his computer inside his home office emailing the mayor. He was trying to find out if he had received his package. A hot cup of cappuccino kept him company while he waited for a response. Jenny walked in wearing oversized pajamas and carrying a cup of coffee in her hand. She sat down Indian style on the sofa.

"Mornin', daddy," Jenny said cheerfully. "You didn't get much sleep last night."

Randy sat his cup down. "Did I wake you?"

Jenny shrugged. "Doesn't matter, I love you no matter what. You can be a sleepwalker for all I care." She stood and strolled over to the bookshelves, running her hand along the rows of books until she found one that sparked her interest. "*Million Dollar Dreams and Federal Nightmares,*" she read out loud. "Nice title."

Randy peered at the book in her hand. "True story. Those young boys got rich in that book, running a dope ring of drugs from L.A to. Atlanta."

Jenny smirked. "Wow, interesting. Guess I'm gonna have to see what it's like for myself."

Leaning back in his comfortable leather chair with his legs

crossed, he kept his eyes locked on her while she thumbed through the book. She seemed to be genuinely infatuated with it. "Drug trafficking fascinates you?" Randy asked.

Jenny placed the book back on the shelf. "Very much."

"I used to do that for a living but I changed and started doing other shit that got me way more money," he told her. "That's how I got where I am today." He took a sip of the hot liquid. "I stole to enrich my life, not to define it."

"For some people, it's exactly the opposite," Jenny replied in a serious tone. "Breakfast?"

"Yes," he replied slowly. His eyes remained on her as she exited the room. It was chilly outside when Randy stepped onto the porch. He fastened his robe then blew hot air into his hands on his way to the mailbox. After he sorted through the mail, he stood there browsing through the latest edition of XXL Magazine.

Olivia watched Randy from where she stood. He looked nothing like what she was used to, yet he was so handsome and athletically built. She hated to have to do to him what had to be done, but he owed a debt to her.

The sound of tires squealing on concrete caused Randy to turn around and he watched Polo's Cadillac pull up at the gate. Randy checked his watch, thinking it was kind of early for him to be there. Something was up. Polo stepped out of the car holding his gun at this side while watching over his shoulder and Randy watched him curiously.

"Mornin'," Randy greeted him.

"Mornin', hell. We got niggas out here looking to take our heads clean the fuck off. Literally." Polo showed him the bruise around his neck and it left a frown plastered to Randy's face.

"What happened?"

"I showed up at City Hall and met the man like you said. Unlike what you said, them honkies made me drive to an alley and tried to off my ass. But I reversed it, you see, 'cause I'm a muthafuckin' trained killa, nigga." He pointed the gun at Randy. "We got to find out what happened and get they ass today. Not tomorrow, nigga, today."

"Be cool, Polo."

"Fuck, cool!" Polo walked away then came back. "Nigga, they tried to kill me!"

"Alright then, Polo. Let's go." Randy started toward the car. "Wait a minute. Where we goin'? Huh?"

"I don't give a fuck. I'll knock the mayor's and the governor's heads clean off then lay down and do my time the right way." He paused for a moment. "On medication." Randy just stared at him, shaking his head.

Randy didn't go to the hotel that night. Instead, he shook Jenny and rented himself a cheap motel room. For the entire night, he sat on the bed smoking rock after rock and drinking vodka. One thing the drug had done that he didn't like was make him weak. Every time his stress level accelerated, he wanted the pipe. Whenever he thought, it was about the pipe. In just a short time, the pipe had taken over his life. And at the moment, there was nothing he could do about it. Nor did he want to.

"Randy," he heard a deep voice say. He dropped the pipe and jumped up.

"Who is it?" he asked.

"Randy," the voice repeated, this time with an echo. Randy picked up his gun and the phone then ran into the closet. He copped a squat on the floor with his gun pointed at the door, ready to unload on whoever came through it. Several terrifying minutes passed but nobody came and the voices stopped. He fished the phone off the floor then dialed Yandy's number. Yandy sounded sleepy when she answered.

"Hello."

"Yandy." His voice was a desperate whisper.

"Randy?"

"I need you to come get me." He cracked the closet door, peeping through it. "They're trying to kill me."

Yandy cut on the lamp and sat up in bed. "Who? Who's trying to kill you?"

"Goddammit, they're trying to kill me. They want me dead." It sounded like he was crying. "If you don't come get me, I'ma gonna ... I'm gonna kill myself," he sniffled. "And my blood will be on your hands."

"Where are you?"

"Oh my God!" Randy yelled.

*Boc! Boc! Boc!*

After Yandy heard the gunshots, the line went dead in her ear. "Hello! Randy! . . . Randy! Damn!" Yandy slammed down the phone just as Morgen walked into the room.

"You okay?" he asked. Yandy tossed the covers to the side then shot past Morgen on her way to the kitchen. "Where're you going?"

"To make some coffee." Morgen moved to the dresser where he opened his laptop, logged on, and began checking his email. His cheeks sagged and a knot formed inside his stomach when he read one message in particular.

*Frankie and Petey were found shot to death in an alley this morning. Polo's still alive. Be careful.*

The glass of Brandy he was holding fell from his hand. He had tried to kill Polo and failed. It was going to be on now. With his crazy ass on the loose, there was no telling what was about to happen.

"Oh my God!" he cried. His original plan was to kill Polo and take the money so the mayor would never receive it, assuming the mayor would become angry and make Randy step down. Then Morgen would step in and take over. Corporate takeovers. That was what he lived for. Now that he had fucked up he didn't know what to expect. He'd have to consult with Madison.

The next morning Yandy woke early. She showered, ate, and dressed in a hurry. Morgen was already at his office so she grabbed her purse and hit the door. Neither on the news nor in the paper did she find anything about a man killing himself. She drove by a few motels but didn't see Randy's car and only Jenny's car was parked in the driveway when she drove by Randy's house. Yandy didn't think it was likely but she drove to the hotel to see if Randy had shown up for work. Surprisingly, his car was parked in his private spot. The elevator ride to his office seemed to take forever. When the door opened, she sprang into the hallway. Randy's secretary was on the phone as Yandy approached her desk.

"Is the boss in?"

"Yes, but he is currently in a meeting." Yandy sighed and took a seat.

Inside Randy's office, he sat on the edge of his desk while the mayor chewed his ass. He badly wanted to excuse himself to take a hit. All he had to do was go to the bathroom but he didn't want to chance hearing that faceless voice inside his head while the mayor was present. The mayor paced the floor with his hands on his hips.

"Goddammit, Randy! We were supposed to keep this quiet."

"I thought we did."

"Then why did I receive that email this morning?"

"What email?"

"Someone, I suppose whoever was responsible for trying to take out your guy, emailed me this morning threatening to go public if you retaliate."

*Who could that be?* he thought. Fredrick or Morgen? Spud wouldn't know how to email anyone, let alone the mayor. Fredrick was on his hit list anyway so that left Morgen. Randy said, "I don't know how someone received word that Polo was leaving here with the money. No one else knew other than you. Yet, he got intercept—" Randy cut his words off.

The mayor was curious. "What's wrong?" While staring down at the waxed floor, Randy spotted the reflection of a red light. He held up his hand, signaling the mayor to be quiet. On his hands and knees, he peered under the desk and spotted a small cassette recorder that was expertly fastened with Velcro. He pulled it out and when the mayor saw the recorder in his hand he freaked out.

"Oh my goodness, someone's on to us." Randy tried to figure out why it was there. As far as he knew, the Feds didn't use cheap equipment so he figured it had to be Morgen's doing. But why? The answer to monitor his business movements came quickly. That's how he knew what Polo was holding and where he was on his way to. Morgen didn't want Randy to keep the casino because he wanted to be in charge. Let Randy, the black fool, build the clientele back up so he could take it over. That was Morgen's plan all along—to steal it back.

"It was Morgen," Randy stated after a lengthy deliberation.

"Morgen? How in the hell do you know that? If word gets out that I'm taking bribes, I'm finished and so are you."

"There's no need for threats, Mr. Mayor."

"You need to fix this, Randy. Now!" He left the office. Randy dropped the recorder on the desk then plopped down in his chair. He needed a hit. He couldn't go up against Morgen; the man had the mob backing him. One phone call to Chicago from Morgen and a hundred unrecognizable men would come looking for him. He examined the recorder. It was the kind you had to possess to listen to it. That ruled Morgen out because he hadn't stepped foot in the office since their argument. That only left one other person . . . Jenny.

Yandy walked through the door, destroying his train of thought. He gazed up at her shocked to see her face.

His secretary followed. "Mr. Randy Harris, we're having problems with the delivery in the food court, the boxing promoter wants you to call him," she said as she placed a stack of papers on his desk, "And I need your signature on these."

"Okay. Have the food court handle the delivery problem."

She nodded then excused herself.

"Hey."

"Hey yourself," Randy said solemnly. Yandy was nervous and felt weird. She had known him forever but today everything felt different.

"What happened the other night?"

"The other night?"

"Yes, you called me the other night saying someone was trying to kill you."

"Wasn't me," he lied.

"It wasn't you?" Her look was accusing.

"No." Randy stood and stepped around his desk and Yandy stood too. As he passed her, she reached out and hugged him tightly and felt his body accepting her embrace. It was a short moment before he pulled away.

Holding onto his hands, she asked, "Where are you going? Talk to me, Randy," she begged.

He avoided all eye contact. "I gotta piss."

"Randy, are you in trouble?"

After a short hiss, he said, "What kind of trouble could I be in?"

"Randy, I'm serious."

"And so am I. Now leave me alone, okay?" He snatched away from her and stepped into the bathroom. The cold water that he splashed on his face felt refreshing. Several deep breaths were taken before he removed his pipe from the cabinet and popping sounds came from the pipe while he sucked on it. When he finally came out some twenty minutes later, Yandy was gone.

## 22

————

"There you go, sucka," Polo said. He was sitting in a stolen car parked in the garage of Fredrick's office. When Fredrick's limo pulled in, Polo pulled his gloves over his hands and checked the chamber of his gun. He watched as Fredrick stepped out of the limo talking on his cell phone while the car pulled away. There was a doorman waiting at the elevator.

"Evening, Fredrick," he said with a smile and Frederick nodded. The doorman keyed the elevator just as Polo started the car, put it in drive, and gunned it in their direction. When the doorman heard the roaring engine, he quickly turned around. "Fredrick!" he shouted. Fredrick turned around, saw the car coming, and froze. Polo hit the brakes and slid dead into them.

*Boom!*

The sounds that escaped their mouths was sickening as blood and saliva splattered the windshield. Polo exited the car with his gun drawn. Fredrick was still conscious but from the waist down they were crushed.

"You tried to kill me," Polo said. Fredrick wasn't able to respond. "Now I'm about to send yo' ass straight to God." Polo raised his weapon. Fredrick looked like he had Parkinson's as he shook uncontrollably.

*Boc! Boc! Boc!*

Polo moved the barrel to the doorman and shot him as well then wiped the car down and fled on foot.

"Tonight I'm having a get together with some friends," Jenny informed Randy. She was stocking their home bar with various bottles of liquor.

"Great," he yawned. "I'm going to bed. Wake me when the party is over." After a long, hot shower, he crawled into bed naked. The silky satin sheets felt good to his skin. He fluffed his pillow and buried his face in it. Not long after, he was snoring. Loud music blasting through the walls of the house woke Randy. His eyes fluttered open as he rose with a frown on his face. He wondered why the hell Jenny was playing the music so damned loud until he heard people chattering. He climbed out of bed and peeped out the door. All sorts of faces he didn't recognize were in his living room partying. Randy hurried into some clothes and went to see what was going on. Women were in the middle of the floor dancing with other women, couples were freaking on the sofas, and the room smelled like weed as cocaine covered the coffee table. There were more white faces than there were black.

Randy fixed himself a drink, positioned himself by the bar, and watched the crowd. Suddenly, he felt a pair of lips on his neck as arms clamped around his waist.

"Hey, baby." The voice belonged to RiRi. "Still mad?"

"Why wouldn't I be? I let you four bitches come along and fuck up my life."

Giggling, RiRi said, "Blame your wife, not me. And you can blame yourself for being so vulnerable and gullible when it comes to her." A long legged, blue eyed white woman with blonde hair sashayed over to them.

"Hi, RiRi," she said with a wide grin. "Who's your friend? Does he party?"

"His name is Randy. He's the husband of the host and owner of this big ass house. And yes, he does party, Julia."

Julia took Randy by the hand. "Well come on, let's the three of us go find a bedroom."

"RiRi, where's Jenny?" he asked.

A short white boy with a long ponytail stood up on the sofa and yelled, "The bar is ours! Owww! Let's have a fuckfest!" He kicked off his shoes.

"Upstairs in the guest room," Julia answered for RiRi and RiRi shot her a look. "Well he asked." Randy took off upstairs, and Julia and RiRi followed.

"Randy, wait!" RiRi yelled. "Listen to me first."

He stopped on the staircase and turned around. "What?"

"Umm, Jenny's high so prepare for the worst." When he busted open the guest room door, he didn't like what he saw. Jenny was naked in the bed, sandwiched between two white boys.

"Randy," Jenny said slowly. Her face was made up like a hooker's and she was stoned.

"You fuckin' tramp!" he hollered. He felt a hand touch his shoulder and looked back. "What?" It was the short, drunk guy that was standing on the sofa getting naked. He had on Randy's robe as he held onto a beer.

"Excuse me, dude," he said, "but I need you to leave my party." He pointed the beer can toward the door.

Randy scowled. "What?"

"Buddy, you're up here tripping over one hoe when there's a whole bunch of hoes downstairs. C'mon, man, let's go get loaded and fuck some of these hoes together, just like they're doing Jenny."

"Yeah," Julia encouraged. "Forget about her and focus on these." She removed her shirt, revealing large breasts and pink, round nipples. RiRi and Judd, the crazy white boy, led him back downstairs. They stopped in front of a group of women.

Judd said, "Now you can have any of them, except for her . . . her . . . that one . . . not Jamie either. You know what, why don't we move to another group? 'Cause all those hoes are mine," he snickered. A redheaded girl with green eyes, body piercings, and a lot of tattoos volunteered. Randy, Julia, RiRi and the new girl went to his bedroom but Judd stayed behind.

"Who wants to play spin the bottle?" he shouted. The redhead, Shania, set out a bunch of coke. After they all got high, they climbed onto the huge bed. Woman on woman, man on woman, and vice versa. They went round after round. When they neared exhaustion, they took a crack break. RiRi loaded the straight shooter so everyone could take a blast. When the high kicked in, it was on again.

*Boom!*

The door flew open and everyone on the bed snapped to attention. Jenny came through the door with a loaded gun in her hand. "Get the fuck outta my room!" she yelled sluggishly. Her eyes were barely visible. The women did as they were told as Randy sat high and spooked. Jenny knew it.

"Jenny," he said as he nervously inched toward her.

"Don't Jenny me, muthafucka. You're up in here fuckin' in our bed?"

"Girl, put the gun down."

Judd walked in. "What the fuck is going on now?" He peered down and saw the gun in her hand. "Oh shit! She got a gun!" he yelled and ran out of the room. While Jenny looked at Judd, Randy tackled her to the floor. They tussled a while before Randy snatched the gun from her hand.

He raised it as if he were about to strike her with it. "Bitch, I oughta knock yo' fuckin' head off," he threatened.

Jenny shielded her face with her arms but she got brave after she realized he wasn't gonna do it. "Do it, you crackhead, coward ass pussy. Up in here screwin' in my bed. You ain't shit!" Jenny shouted. "You hear me?" He grabbed her arm and snatched her up on her feet. She tried to break free but it was no use.

"I'm tired of your shit, bitch," he said while dragging her through the house. The startled crowd made a hole for the fighting couple to get through. The guests in the house were regular swingers and had never witnessed such a thing go on between a couple.

"Let me go, you fucking bastard!" Jenny clawed at his arms but he still wouldn't release his grip. The cold night air smacked her in the face as soon as the door opened. All she wore was a nightgown so chill bumps quickly spread over her flesh. Her attitude instantly changed to a soft plea. "Baby, please don't throw me out. It's cold out here."

"Too late, bitch, you gettin' the fuck outta here," he growled. He tucked the gun inside his drawers then slung her off the porch. When she still refused to leave, he fired two shots over her head.

*Boc! Boc!*

"Bitch, I said leave," Randy said coldly then closed the door. Soon after, she heard the music come back on.

"Okay, muthafucka. I got something for yo' ass."

An hour later, Randy sat on the sofa between Shania and Julia, bent over the table and shoveling coke up his nose. He had gotten so high when he tried to snort another line the powder fell right back out. He had fallen in love with the girl, but it wasn't quite as good as the rock. Everybody in the house was dancing, laughing, and having a good time until . . .

*Boom! Boom! Boom!*

"It's the police! Open up!"

Judd was the first to jump up. "Oh my fuckin' God! Raid!" Everybody, including Randy, started picking up dope, pipes, bags, and whatever else they could find and dashed to the four bathrooms. The cops heard all the movement going on inside the house and asked Jenny for permission to enter which she granted it. Upon entering the residence, they didn't know who to grab first. The entire scene was chaotic. Naked people were running around everywhere. To uncomplicate the situation, they set out to find the owner of the house. When they found him, he was in his bedroom bathroom, breaking up a crack pipe but he had already flushed the dope. He was arrested for domestic violence and possession of drug paraphernalia. Jenny stood in the doorway with her hands on her hips, smiling deviously while they carried him away.

"I'm here to bail out Randy Harris," Polo said at the front desk. "I'll be paying cash."

"That'll be twenty-five hundred dollars," the bailiff informed him as he placed a clipboard on the counter in front of him. "Sign here." After everything was processed, Polo waited for Randy outside. He sat in the car grooving to a JAY-Z CD when he saw Randy come out.

"Thanks, man," Randy said. Polo mugged the side of his head while smoke flowed out his nostrils. Randy said, "What?"

"What the hell you doing in the house with a bunch of crack pipes and naked white people?" Randy was too embarrassed to admit the truth. Polo sighed. "Don't tell me that bitch caught you smoking crack and turned you in?"

"Take me home." Randy took his Blackberry out the sack as Polo put the car in drive.

"I took care of our Fredrick problem."

"I know. Seen it on the news."

"Fucked 'em up, didn't I?" Randy nodded. "Un huh. I told you I don't play that shit."

"That's good. The detectives came to speak to me about ole Freddy. Said they were supposed to meet with him this morning."

"They probably thought you had something to do with his murder."

"Yeah, now he don't have nothing to tell 'em." Polo hit his cigarette. "Morgen's next on my shit list. Fuck what ya heard. His ass is out 'cause somebody tried to kill me."

## 23

Yandy, Spud, and Chuck were at Spud's place preparing to hit the hotel. Randy wouldn't know what hit him until it was over, but it wouldn't take him long to figure it out because he knew who he snaked. His friends. And they were the best thieves he had ever known. The amateur boxing bout was going on at the casino that night so chances were they wouldn't even be noticed. If for some reason they were, the guns would come out and they would either kill or be killed.

Spud looked at his watch. "Where the hell is Big Boi?"

Yandy placed her gun in her waist. "He should be pulling up at the jewelry store any minute." Spud took a minute to admire the way Yandy looked in her black trousers and security shirt as her ponytail brought out her face. She saw him eyeing her, but ignored him.

Chuck walked into the kitchen carrying three Point Blank vests and tossed one to each of them. "It's time."

Yandy took two steps before Spud clutched her arm. She looked down at his hand then at his face. "What?"

"You okay?"

She studied his face. "I'm fine. Why?"

He shrugged. "You look kinda funny, that's all." He released his grip and Yandy walked away.

An hour or so later, the armored truck pulled into the parking lot of the grocery store before two of the guards got out the back and walked inside. Spud and Chuck were browsing through cereal in aisle D when they saw the guards pass their aisle as they headed toward the back room. Five minutes later the door opened back up. One of the guards came out with a pistol drawn by his side. His eyes scanned the area for possible ambushers then, after the signal, the guard carrying the money bags came out.

Spud and Chuck moved quickly. From their blind side, they stepped forward and produced two stun guns. Before the guards knew what hit them, they were on their knees, shaking uncontrollably. One dropped his gun and the other dropped the bags. The two thieves picked up the bags and gun then raced for the exit. At almost the exact same time, Yandy stopped the stolen Chevy next to the armored car. The driver had his eyes locked on the store entrance so he didn't see her chuck the can of tear gas through the window on the passenger side. Seconds later he leapt from the truck, gagging and coughing as he fell to the ground. Yandy was sitting behind the wheel of the truck when Spud and Chuck came out of the store. They jumped inside and she pulled off. The Highway was just down the road and it was a straight shot to the hotel.

"Don't get any of that oatmeal on your shirt, Cindy," Madison said to his daughter as he sat at the breakfast table reading the newspaper. His wife, Shelby, fixed his plate and sat it in front of him. "Bacon and a boiled egg," he said as he put the paper down. "Yummy."

Shelby smiled. "You don't need to go to work full. Besides, I'm supporting the removal of that pouch you're growing." Cindy found that humorous.

"Oh, you think that's funny, huh? You all just hurt daddy's feelings, I want y'all to know that." Shelby and Cindy looked at one another then stood and walked around the table to sandwich hug their king.

"We're sorry, honey," Shelby said and kissed him.

"Yeah, dad, we're sorry. We're gonna make it up to you by taking you to dinner and a movie tonight."

"Dinner and a movie? I'd love that. Your mother and I haven't done that since the seventies. Back then we used to—"

"Please spare her the details," Shelby said. "Time for you to go."

"Damn, already?" He stood and walked to the front room. He holstered his Glock, hugged and kissed his family, then walked out the door. Madison waved and smiled before he drove off. On his way to work, he started thinking. How did we come to this point in the investigation? Law had told him he obtained the information from one of his informants. *What informant? And where did that informant suddenly obtain information about Spud's crew? What professionals would tell somebody about a joint they were casing before they took it down? Doesn't add up. Could Law be dirty? I was once upon time* Madison thought. As he headed out, he figured it was worth looking in to.

Inside the garage of the police station, Madison, Law, and six members of their task force geared up for combat. Their destination was the jewelry store on the plaza. Madison and Law drove a blue Ford Crown Victoria followed by the black task force van. They arrived at the scene before Big Boi did and posted around the back of the building across the street. From the roof of the building, Madison scanned the entire area through binoculars. Like any other day, people were walking by, heading to the nearby restaurants and shopping stores.

"Where the hell are those sons of bitches? Law, I thought your informant said they're supposed to be here." "Relax. He said they'd be there so they'll be here." Madison lit a cigarette. "I'd like to know how he knows so much." Law ignored the question just like Madison figured he would. A white Astro van pulled in front of the jewelry store, blocking Madison's view before the driver disappeared to the back. They couldn't see the other side of the van but they knew someone was exiting out the side door. "It's them," Madison said.

"Let's go." Law jumped up, but Madison held him down.

"Don't move. Wait just a moment." Madison's eyes remained on the van. He glanced at his watch to time the robbery as Law pretended to be impatient.

"C'mon, man."

"Man, sit your ass down." The next time he looked at his watch four minutes had passed. Too long for a professional robbery, yet the van was still there. "Something's wrong. Don't you think, Law?"

"I . . . I . . ."

"Move in," Madison said into his radio. Big Boi was standing at the counter inside the jewelry store holding a platinum necklace when the police stormed in. "Get down! Police!" Big Boi and the clerk heard the word "police" and immediately got down on the floor. Madison and Law entered the store after the area was secured and Madison didn't like what he saw. It didn't look like a robbery or anything else had gone down. He kneeled next to Big Boi.

"Tell me what's going on, Big Boi?" Madison asked. "That is your name, isn't it?"

"Yes, but I'm just picking up a necklace for my girl," Big Boi explained. Madison fired up a cigarette, thought for a moment, then threatened to put it out in Big Boi's face. Big Boi flinched.

"I know what's going on here, Big Boi," Madison said. "Somewhere at this very moment, there's a 211 taking place, and you, pal, were used as a decoy to throw us off. It would've worked except for one thing."

Madison pointed two fingers at Big Boi's eyes. "Your eyes, Big Boi. They're unique."

"What're you talking about?" Big Boi demanded.

"I know a bank owner named Morgen. He showed us a video of one of his banks getting robbed," Madison lied. "In that video footage, we spotted a masked man. His eyes were green and brown, just like yours. We would've dismissed it until we found your face in our computer files. No one knows about this but me and my partner. We can keep a lid on it considering you help us locate your friends. If not, you go down for murdering a cop." Madison smiled. "What do ya say?" Law stood by quietly sweating bullets.

**24**

---

The casino was crowded. Plus, the city wasn't accustomed to
hosting fights so it was a big turnout. Meaningless lightweight fights were going on, paving the way for the
upcoming main event. A lot of money was pouring into the hotel that
night. All the suites were booked and the count room was full. There
was so much chaos the president could walk in and go unnoticed.
Polo was in charge of keeping the promoters happy until Randy
arrived and it wasn't hard with the assistance of Freeda, RiRi, Sasha,
and Jenny. With them around, dressed as they were, it was hard for
anyone to concentrate on the fights. Wearing a blue pinstriped suit,
scarf, brim hat, and Gucci framed glasses, Polo sat ringside between
the promoters. He chewed on an unlit cigar, enjoying his moment as
acting manager. The lightweight division champion, Don Deal,
pummeled his contender, Jay Rivers in the fifth round. The crowd
leapt to their feet cheering as

Polo threw down his cigar because from the looks of things he
was about to lose five thousand. "Get yo' gay ass up!" he screamed.
While the crowd was on its feet, Jenny checked her watch. Sasha saw
her then checked hers as well before they nodded to one another.
Jenny excused herself.

"Where you going?" Polo asked.

Jenny stopped in her tracks and answered without turning around. "To the restroom."

Randy shaved his face and head, showered, and put on a tuxedo then draped himself with some of his best jewelry. While he waited for his limo to arrive, the monkey started pounding on his back. The crack was calling him but he had neither crack nor pipe. He was already out front when his car showed up and the driver got out to get the door for him. Randy gazed into his eyes for any signs of a fellow user, but the driver shot Randy a look like he was either crazy or gay.

"Yes?" the driver asked in a feminine voice and Randy's eyes widened.

"Nothing. Sorry, I thought I recognized you." He got inside.

"A closet Gump," the driver said then closed the door with his ass.

Randy finally arrived at the hotel to meet and greet the boxing promoters and thanked the girls for helping to keep the promoters happy while he was away. Ronald Isley was on stage performing a song before the main event but Jenny had not returned. The lights came on and Randy took a seat next to Polo. They whispered a few things in each other's ears before the waitress showed up with a message for Randy.

*Meet me in suite 405. Now. I need to apologize. Love, Jenny.*

Randy leaned toward the promoter and whispered, "Excuse me for a minute, please."

"Sure. Make sure you're around for the after party," he laughed and pointed a jeweled finger at him.

RiRi touched Randy as he walked past and he looked at her. "Watch yourself tonight, Randy. Okay?" He nodded thoughtfully and continued to walk away.

Randy used his master key to open the door to suite 405. Music was playing softly as he cautiously crossed the doorway. The table was set, candles were lit, and a bottle of champagne chilled inside an ice bucket. Jenny appeared out of nowhere looking stunning in a red evening gown, diamond earrings, high heeled stilettos, and a rose in her hand. Slowly, she stepped over to him and Randy took a step back.

"This shit ain't gon' work this time."

Continuing toward him, Jenny said, "Naw, Randy. This time I'ma take a different approach, you'll see."

"Bitch, you put me in jail," he reminded her.

Jenny stopped about a foot away from him. "Is that all? What else have I done to you, Randy?" She looked at the champagne. "Wait a minute, hold that thought. Let me fix you a drink first." Jenny sat at the table across from Randy sipping champagne. "You were saying, Randy?"

"Ever since I met you, I've been fucked up. I did everything I could for you. I bought you everything you wanted. So I had to kick your ass a few times, what choice did I have? I was hoping to knock some sense into your stubborn ass. For a while, you'd act like everything was all good then suddenly, here comes the bullshit again. I'm sick of this shit." Jenny sat there with a triumphant smirk on her face and Randy couldn't understand why. That look almost put fear in him.

"What does all that sound like to you, Randy?" she asked. "Doesn't it all sound like child's play? Hmm? The beautiful young girl gets everything she wants, yet she's still unsatisfied. Why? Because she feels like it's all owed to her anyway. You catch the little tramp screwing in the house. What do you do? You spank her. After the spanking wears off, little girlie goes back to being mischievous again." Randy stared at her curiously. The conversation was headed someplace. He just didn't know where.

Yandy pulled the armored truck up to the hotel, and Chuck and Spud walked inside looking like guards. They walked in flashing their badges on their way to the count room. Spud put the card into the slot and the door opened. The gamblers inside The Den were busy doing their own thing and the employees were busy running the tables and serving drinks. To them, it looked like a routine money pick up. The counters inside the count room already had four bags packed with money that was ready to go. Spud was in awe of the room as the counters sat on straight back chairs and counted the money on clear glass tables. There were steel shelves and floors to bear the tons of cash and coins. Bills of tens, twenties, and hundreds were sorted into one inch thick ten thousand dollar bricks stacked on the shelves against the wall. A sign posted on the wall read:

*A million dollars in hundreds weighs twenty and a half pounds, twenties weigh one hundred and two pounds, and fives weigh four hundred and eight pounds.*

Spud guessed it to be guidelines for them to follow. The two counters in the room saw the guards pull guns and immediately stopped counting money. They stood and stepped away from the tables.

"No questions," Spud said. "Take out some more of those black bags and start filling them until we tell you to stop." The counters did as they were told. Chuck started lugging bags out to the truck, two at a time, starting with the four that were ready. Yandy nervously glanced around while she waited but seeing Chuck rush out with the two bags gave her some relief. He loaded them into the back, then left again, returning with two more. Before she knew it, he had loaded eight bags into the back of the truck. She pointed at her watch and Chuck acknowledged her signal then strolled back inside. Yandy sat up to get a look at the bags in the back through the little window. When she stood, the cell phone Law gave her in case he needed to alert her fell between the seats.

"Yes!" she said excitedly. She didn't hear her phone vibrating over the sound of the loud truck. Law had sent her a text.

*Abort!*

"We have a 211 in progress at the casino!" Yandy heard the announcement over the scanner inside the truck.

"Oh, shit!" She got on her radio. "Spud, get out of there! Now!" She put the truck in second gear, waiting to take off. "C'mon, c'mon, c'mon." Inside the count room, Spud was helping fill four more bags when he heard Yandy on his radio.

"Let's go!" Spud commanded. Yandy looked at the doors and still didn't see her partners but loud sirens wailed close by. She pulled off just as Madison and Law hit the corner. Law saw the ass end of the truck going up the road and smiled lightly, thanking the Lord his son would get a chance at life. Spud and Chuck walked out the building as Madison slowly he pulled into the entrance, glancing around.

Spud spotted Madison's car before he saw them. "Go! Go!" They took off running to a green Ford Bronco they had parked in the east parking area. After they got inside, Chuck removed an AR-15 from under the seat and Spud bolted out the parking spot. Madison heard the tires squealing and turned his head in their direction. The Bronco was coming at them full speed. Hurriedly, Madison sped forward to get out the way. Spud turned right out onto the street, damn near tipping the Bronco over and Madison threw his car in reverse, backing all the way out onto the street then took off after them. The whole episode left Law trying to figure out what the hell was going on.

Two left hooks and an overhand right to the jaw sent the champ down for the count and the crowd was on its feet. Everybody in the house seemed to be upset except for Polo who was jumping up and down.

"Take his muthafuckin head off!" Polo shouted. "Ha! Ha!" The promoters were all in stunned silence while the referee counted. The champ slowly climbed to his feet and the fight resumed after a slow four count. Sasha stood and excused herself then seconds later RiRi did the same. Freeda waited until the crowd got hype again before she snuck out.

"Hey, man, where did the women go?" one of the promoters asked.

Polo said, "What? Man, fuck them hoes. I'm about to win fifty thousand."

Sasha led the girls to the linen closet then unlocked and opened the door. "We've got to move fast before the fight is over." Each girl changed into a pair of trousers, black T-shirt, bulletproof vests, and a ski mask. RiRi passed out the guns to each of them as Sasha looked at her watch.

"Show time," she announced as she pulled the mask over her face. The gamblers inside The Den were having a good time and the fight was being shown on the big screens. According to Sasha's watch, the armored truck guards had just left. Four guards were posted in The Den while majority of security was busy covering the fight. The security guards in the camera room upstairs were so busy watching the fight like everyone else they didn't see the three women carrying guns through the casino. Suzie, the bartender, had took the guards on duty some non-alcoholic beverages about five minutes earlier but they found themselves nodding and sick. Sasha stormed in holding an AK-47 in the air and Suzie cut the music.

"Everybody line up against the wall, now!" Sasha ordered. "Don't fuck with me!" Suzie politely relieved the paralyzed guards of their guns and walkie-talkies. They were bound by their own cuffs. The gamblers and dealers all did as they were told. Wallets, jewelry, purses, and everything else of value was ordered to be thrown on the floor. Freeda and RiRi used plastic zip ties to bind everybody's hands behind their backs. Sasha checked her watch again then waited for the word from upstairs.

"What's up with you, Jenny?" Randy inquired.

Jenny nodded toward a package sitting in front of Randy. "Open it," she said. "Tell me what you think." Randy cautiously picked up the package and opened it. It was a photograph inside of a platinum frame. The picture stopped his heart as a jolt shot through his body. He could not believe what he was seeing, but now that he thought about it, it should've been obvious. "You didn't see it because you're blind, baby," Jenny said. "All you see is Randy Harris." The photograph was of Olivia holding up two graduation certificates. There standing next to her with her arm around her, smiling proudly, was none other than Jenny. The name Olivia was written across the photograph right above the word forever. "Aren't you proud of me, daddy? I graduated from high school with honors. Unfortunately, mama graduated from drug rehab. It's a good place. I strongly recommend it for you if you ever plan on kicking your habit."

*No wonder I was so drawn to her* Randy thought. *She's my seed.* His face wrinkled. "But we... we—"

"Never. We never had sex, you only thought we did. You couldn't tell the difference when I would sneak out of bed and let RiRi take my place. That's because you're blind, daddy," she shrugged. "Although I would have done it to do what I'm about to do."

"You hid the tape recorder in my office? Why?"

"I wanted Morgen to kill Polo so I wouldn't have to deal with him trying to protect you. I listened to the tape while you were in the bathroom that day." Jenny lifted her dress and pulled the gun that was strapped to her leg then flipped open her cell phone. "I'm on my way down."

"So, why go through all this?" Randy asked.

"I took you through everything you took my mother through and got to know my daddy at the same time. Got treated like the child I missed out on being. You whooped me and spoiled me but now it's time for me to collect my back child support."

Randy cracked a smile. "You're gonna try to rob my casino?"

"Not try, daddy. It's already happening right now so get the fuck up!" She pointed the gun toward him.

"I have to admit, I'm impressed," he said as he stood. "Which way?"

"To your office, now!" Jenny followed Randy to his office. He fumbled with his keys at the door, trying to figure out what he could do. He peered over his shoulder at her as the barrel of the gun was pointed at his back. The look in her eyes was cold. The door unlocked and they stepped inside. Randy looked at her. "Now, I want the security pass to the count room," Jenny demanded.

"I don't—"

"I bugged your office, remember, daddy? Cut the lies." Randy reluctantly walked to the safe and opened it. "You're already dead to me, daddy," she said, "so don't think for one moment I won't lay your ass down." He handed over the card, and Jenny led him back to the suite where she cuffed him to the tub and gagged his mouth then took the elevator to The Den.

One of the security guards inside the camera room finally came to and examined the screens. He gasped when he saw what was going on inside The Den and snatched up the phone.

"Don't do that." His partner drew his gun on him. "Put down the phone and watch the fight." After he put down the phone, his partner relieved him of his firearm.

Jenny put on her mask before she entered the casino. The girls had everybody in line so she walked straight over to the count room door as RiRi stood beside her. After the door opened, they stormed in with guns drawn. She saw all the empty shelves and what was left of the money scattered over the table and floors. The grunting they heard led them to the other side of the table where they found the counters bound and gagged. RiRi pulled the tie out one of their mouths.

"What happened here?" A man looked up at the masked woman through pleading eyes.

"The armored guards robbed us." Jenny didn't know what to think. It was a hell of a coincidence that someone decided to rob the casino on the exact same night.

*Unfuckingbelievable.* She put on her heels and left the room. "Hold it down," she instructed as she took the elevator up to the security room. Her inside security guard saw her coming and let her in.

"What's happening?"

"I need you to roll back about fifteen minutes of tape." The man rewound the tape and they watched as the two armored guards entered the hotel. The two men seemed to keep their faces out of the camera's view. That right there told Jenny they were familiar with the hotel's security system but what really caught her eye was the unique swagger the short one walked with. He was the same height and weight as Spud. "I should've known." Jenny left the room and headed back to Randy.

Randy fell backward but the cuffs wouldn't allow him to go anywhere. Jenny removed the stuffing from his mouth, squeezed his jaws until his lips parted like a fish, and jammed her gun inside his mouth.

"Your friends stole my money and I want it back." She kneed him in the balls.

"Owww!"

"You knew about this, didn't you?" She kicked him in the face.

"No!"

"Liar!" she yelled. "Give me my money! You owe that to me!" She took out her phone. "Move out!" Jenny removed the cuffs and forced him to walk. They rode the service elevator down to the kitchen where they walked outside to the back parking lot. The girls were waiting in a van. "That was a neat trick, daddy," Jenny said as she closed the door.

"I swear I don't—"

"Shut up!" Sasha screamed while driving. "Where's the money?"

"Yeah," Freeda said.

Jenny shoved the pistol in Randy's face. "Somebody's a little slicker than we thought. Did he pull the videotapes?"

"Yes."

"Good. I don't want nobody to be able to ID us."

"I can," Randy said.

Jenny smirked. "But you won't. Trust me."

The fight ended just as the girls pulled off. The champ went down in the ninth round and it was the second upset of the night. The promoters didn't appear to be happy about it either. They had lost a fortune betting on the champ. Polo suggested they all go to The Den and have drinks on him. To their surprise, policemen, detectives, and paramedics were crawling all over the place. A crowd of people stood amongst a group of officers making statements. One of the employees informed Polo of the situation, and he immediately got on the phone in an attempt to contact Randy.

## 25

S pud sped through the park, going way too fast for the curvy road. Chuck peered out the back window and saw the Crown Victoria on their ass.

"What're we gonna do?" Chuck asked.

"Whatever you do, don't—"

*Pow! Pow! Pow! Pow!*

Chuck fired shots at the police. It was at that moment Spud felt like he was going to die. He had planned to avoid violence unless absolutely necessary. Bullets covered Madison's front windshield and he veered to the right then back left, damn near bumping the curb.

*Pow! Pow! Pow! Pow!*

*Pop! Pop! Pop! Pop!*

*Pow! Pow! Pow!*

*Pop! Pop!*

Law returned fire as Madison fought for control of the wheel while dodging bullets. The windshield had so many holes through it that it was useless. Spud drove down the street and rounded the corner by a lake. For a brief moment, the truck was on two wheels. About a block before he would have jumped on the highway, he saw that the road was fenced off. Orange and yellow *Caution* and *Road*

*Closed* signs cluttered the road. He wanted to run through the fencing but there was a big hole in the road on the other side. Left with no other choice, Spud hit the brakes.

Spud couldn't see himself just giving up. Thirty to life in federal prison didn't sound too tempting so he turned the truck around. When Madison's car rounded the bend, Spud took off, driving toward them.

"What the—" Madison covered his face, preparing for the collision.

*Blam!*

The big Bronco slammed into the Crown Victoria. Spud kept his foot on the gas, forcing the smaller car backward and smoke came from all eight of their tires.

*Errrrrrrrrk!*

When Law and Madison collected themselves, they kicked out the windshield and fired at the Bronco.

*Pop! Pop! Pop!*

Chuck caught two in the neck, killing him instantly. A bullet pierced Spud's left shoulder and grazed his ear but he put the Bronco in four-wheel drive and continued to force the car backward.

"C'mon you, muthafuckas!" he shouted. "C'mon you, p—" Madison fired a shot that hit Spud right in the nose then another to his head. Spud's dead hands released the wheel and his foot slid off the gas pedal. When the cops finally stopped the car, they rushed the Bronco with their guns drawn. The two men inside the truck were dead. Law found the bags of money in the backseat as Madison called it in on his radio. Law picked up Chuck's hand that still had a loose grip on the gun.

"Hey, Madison, check this out. I found something," Law lied.

"What is—"

*Pop! Pop! Pop!*

Madison held his leaking torso as he fell on the concrete. He could hear his lungs straining for air and then he heard sirens. Help was on the way. Law quickly lugged one of the money bags into the woods. By the time he came back, the police had hit the scene. Two of them were kneeling over Madison.

"The ambulance is on the way," one of them informed him as Law walked up.

"I'm Detective Law. This is my partner. One of those dead assholes got a shot off when we rushed the truck."

"Where are you coming from?"

Law, breathing rapidly, looked at the woods. "Uh, I couldn't get a signal on my phone here so I started walking until I picked up one."

"Why didn't you just use the radio?"

He shrugged. "Shaken up. Wasn't thinking, I guess. I found the bag of money in the back seat."

The men peered through the back window at the single bag. "Great."

Law peered down at Madison who was staring back up at him while taking quick, shallow breaths. He was trying to hold on, but it was his time to go. When Madison finally closed his eyes, he slipped away into the unknown.

Randy had to admit the girls were well organized. Their hideout was a small house that sat in the pit of a dead-end street. RiRi backed the van into an opened garage as Olivia stood inside the garage. Randy looked away from her and Olivia sneered, shocked to see him instead of a van filled with moneybags.

"Where's the money?"

"Somebody beat us to it. Step out, Randy." Randy did as told with blood stains on the front of his suit and face. His lips and nose were swollen. Though she shouldn't have, Olivia felt sorry for him.

"What happened?" Sasha inquired.

On their way into the house, Jenny explained everything. Her theory was Randy somehow caught onto her plan and robbed his own hotel before they could, but Randy denied it all. They led him to an empty room where Jenny kicked him in the back of the knees. When he fell to the floor, she whacked him across the head with the gun. Jenny stared down on him coldly as her chest heaved. "Tie his ass up." Olivia sat on the bed in the other room when Jenny stormed in, wiping blood from her face. She stripped the dress off then put on some pants, a jacket, and a pair of boots. She felt her mother eyeballing her and she sighed.

"What, mother?"

"Can I talk to him?"

Jenny pinned her hair back in the mirror then gazed at her mother. "Sure." Randy sat on the floor against the wall with his hands cuffed behind his back. Olivia walked in and looked down at him.

"Your daughter's out of control but it's your fault. You, her own father, threatened to kill her when she was a baby. Then you killed her uncle, my little brother, in cold blood. In cold blood, Randy . . . right in front of us."

Randy spit blood on the floor. "Bitch, you had me locked away for fifteen fuckin' years. I paid my debt."

"Even under the gun, you're still the same ole Randy Harris." Tears glazed Olivia's eyes. "Paid for what, Randy? For what you owe us? You killed my brother!" she yelled.

She kneeled and could feel his breath on her face. "You fucked my friends and family. You beat me in front of my own daughter. Even through all your evil shit; the name calling, the beatings, the put downs, I still loved you. Sometimes, I think I still do." Jenny listened through the cracked door, growing angrier by the second. Randy used the wall to push himself up, and Olivia stepped back as he stepped toward her. She was nervous while she stared into his cold eyes.

"You still love me, huh?" He attempted to kiss her but she turned her head.

"You drove me to drugs, Randy," she admitted.

Randy stepped back, laughing loudly. "I drove you to drugs? You oughta see what that treacherous daughter of ours did to me. I get so fuckin' spooked when I'm at the pipe I scare the hell out my own goddamn self. I didn't deserve that."

"Neither did I. But you—"

Jenny and her girls stormed into the room. "Enough of the lovey dovey shit." Jenny stared Randy down. "I got you, pops." Jenny peered over his shoulder at RiRi and nodded. She walked in carrying a chair and a phone. She placed the chair behind Randy, and he held still while his daughter sniffed his neck. At one time it would have turned him on but now it was downright disgusting. He wanted to puke when she attempted to kiss him.

"Ah!" Randy fell back in the chair after a knee to the nuts. She threw the phone at his chest. "We're about to play a game that's very familiar to you, daddy. Call your bitch Yandy and tell her to bring me my money." She snatched the gun out of her waist. "Or you're a dead daddy."

"You'd stoop to my level and kill your own flesh over some paper?"

"Yes. See, you stole to enrich your life, but I steal to define mine. It's who I am," she laughed. "Look at what I came from. Two thieving ass crackhead parents." Her girls laughed. "Call her. Now!"

"She won't do it," he explained.

"Then you will die."

"Tiffany Harris," Olivia called. "Please!"

Tiffany peered at her mother through narrow slits. "Get out of here, mother." Sasha led Olivia into the other room. She gazed over her shoulder at Randy one last time before she was rushed out.

"Alright, I'll call her," Randy said as his hands shook while dialing the number.

Randy's memory reflected to the night Jenny asked him if he would have really killed his own daughter. Now he wished he would have lied. She had him in the same situation and he was terrified. He now imagined how she felt at six years old.

Yandy had transferred the moneybags to a rented Dodge Magnum. She was flying down the highway going south when she heard her phone ring. "Spud?" she answered with hopefulness.

"No, Yandy, this is Randy." His voice was full of stress. Yandy didn't miss it.

"What's going on?"

Jenny snatched the phone from him. "Look, bitch, I'm not gonna beat around the bush. You got my money and I want it. If I don't get it, I will shoot this muthafucka in the head then send the picture to your phone. I know you love him, Yandy, let's just see how much." She kicked Randy in the shin. "This isn't a joke so don't assume it is. You have two minutes to call this number back with an answer." Jenny hung up.

Yandy glanced at the clock while she continued south on the highway. Her plan was to go to Texas and start over. She kept telling herself the whole thing was a setup and to keep moving but the thought of someone actually killing Randy haunted her. With half a minute left, Yandy made up her mind. She hit the brakes and pulled over on the shoulder. With uncertainty still lingering, she redialed the number of her last incoming call.

"Hello."

"Where do we meet?"

Several times along the highway Yandy told herself to stop and finish what she had started. *Go to Texas. Start a new life.* But she was Randy's loyal follower. The whole thing could have been a hoax for him to get his money back. If it was, then one good thing would come out of all of this. It would prove to Randy just how much she really loved him.

"Time's up, daddy." Olivia sat on the living room couch nervously rocking back and forth. Now that tit had come down to the wire she was no longer eager to kill him. Just as Jenny placed the gun to Randy's temple the phone rung.

"Hello."

"Where do we meet?"

"You're just like my mother, a damned fool. I married him and still don't get it." She peered down at Randy. "Meet us at Lookout Point in thirty minutes and come alone." Jenny slammed the phone down. "Your bitch is gonna come through." Randy felt a sense of relief come over him. After all he had put her through, he wouldn't expect her to throw piss on him if he were on fire. Freeda and Sasha escorted Randy back out to the van. Jenny grabbed her shades off the table as Olivia sipped Scotch.

"Tiffany," Olivia called.

Jenny didn't look at her. "What, mother?"

"Don't hurt your daddy. We've hurt him enough."

"Have we? He paid us for all the pain we've suffered because of him? The depression? The loneliness I felt while you were strung out, chasing your next hit? The proms, dances, and field trips I missed? I had to steal maxi pads and deodorant just so the girls at school would stop teasing me 'cause I stunk." She took a breath. "But it made me tough and independent." She finally looked down at her mother. "I used that bastard to get back everything I had missed out on. Material things, love, even whoopings . . . but I still spent quality time with my daddy." Jenny held up her gun. "Now it's time to collect my dues, mama. After tonight, there will be no looking back."

Olivia stood and hugged her daughter. "I love you, Jenny, and I understand but I think we've done enough," she whispered in her ear. "Let it go. Randy will hunt us down if we don't kill him and I can't live my life like that. I made a promise to the Lord that I would change if he got me off that evil narcotic and he did." Olivia's words only angered Jenny.

"Mother, you're a weak coward and you have always been one." Jenny squeezed the trigger.

*Pow!*

"Uhhh!" Olivia fell onto the couch holding her bleeding stomach. Shock and fear covered her face as she peered up at her demon of a daughter. Jenny's eyes were cold orbs as she stood there waiting for her mother to die. At first, she wondered how her daddy could think about killing his own blood. Now she learned that it felt no different than killing a stranger.

"Before I see you turn on me, mother, I would rather see you dead in your grave." She kissed her on the lips. "Goodbye, mama. I love you." Jenny left her mother there to die alone.

Randy stared out of the van window with Jenny sat next to him. She could just about imagine what was going through his mind. The great thief had been gotten by his own spawn. The very creature that slept with him every night and sealed their vows with a kiss on an exotic island. His own seed turned him out on crack and ghost pussy, and now she was about to escape with his bankroll.

Jenny spoke, "I remember when I was a kid, you, mother, and I were having a barbeque at the house. Everybody was having a good time until mother caught you doin' it in the bathroom with her cousin. She tried to kill herself that night. That's why you caught me in the bed with those two dudes. How did it feel?"

Randy licked his lips. "It hurt," he admitted. "I learned a helluva lesson fuckin' with you, Je—Tiffany."

"Mother was a good woman."

Randy thought curiously. "You didn't—"

"No." She fired up a cigarette. "She killed herself. Doesn't matter. She was sick anyway," she lied. "I guess she only wanted to live long enough to see you get yours." She blew smoke in his face. "Cigarette?"

Randy sneered. "You fuckin'—"

Jenny slapped him across the face. "Watch your mouth. That's no way to speak to a lady." Jenny thought about something. "Hey, how do you think Yandy would feel if she caught you high?"

Yandy arrived at the meeting place and drove into the circular parking area. The white van was parked facing her direction but she didn't see any people inside. She parked beside it and exited as Jenny appeared out of nowhere with a chrome handgun protruding from her waist. She wore that slick ass smirk on her face.

"Hi," Jenny said. "I'm Tiffany Harris, Randy's daughter."

Yandy's mouth fell open. "Tiffany? How could you—"

"I'll do whatever it takes as long as I'm greatly compensated for it. I got that from my daddy. Where's the money?"

Yandy nodded toward the Magnum. "In the back." Jenny opened the hatch and four bags were in the trunk. She searched each one of them.

"This all of it?" Jenny inquired.

"Yes, Spud and Chuck went their own way with their split."

Smiling, Jenny said, "Tiffany, you pulled it off." She jammed two fingers inside her mouth and whistled. Sasha and Freeda came up the hill with Randy, and Yandy could look at him and tell he was high on something. His eyes were wide open, his lips trembled, and he was constantly looking around. Her first thought was that they had drugged him but Jenny had only given him a loaded pipe, knowing he wouldn't be able to resist. She wanted Yandy to see him at his worst. To see he really wasn't worth saving at all. "Load the bags into the van," Jenny commanded her crew. She stared at Yandy and Randy for a moment then gave him a big hug. "Thank you," she said. She climbed inside the van and drove away.

When the van was gone, Randy stood there avoiding eye contact with Yandy.

"I'm sorry," he said pathetically.

"Sorry my ass. You owe me!" Yandy's hard face softened. "I only did it because I love your stank ass." Randy was acting jumpy. "Did they drug you?"

It took him a moment to answer. "No, I drugged myself. I let Tiffany get me strung out on crack." Yandy didn't know what to say.

All that was left to do was for her to hug him. He hugged her back, and for the first time, he cried in her arms.

"It's okay. We're gonna get you some help, alright?" Yandy gently rubbed his back. "Let's go."

RiRi sat low in the front seat of Jenny's Camaro. She was parked nearby with a fully loaded TEC-9, waiting on Yandy's Magnum to come up the hill. When the Magnum's headlights came into view, RiRi started the car and let down the window. Slowly, the wagon crept in her direction. *Twenty feet. Fifteen feet. Ten feet.* She could see both their heads sitting in the front seat. RiRi bolted out the parking spot, crashing into the wagon and pushing it back against another parked car. Quickly, she hopped out and jogged around to the passenger side of the Magnum. Randy's head bobbled as blood seeped from the top of it. He stared up at her dumbfounded.

RiRi drew the TEC but after all she and Randy had been through she couldn't find it in her heart to pull the trigger. Just as she began lowering her weapon, there was a loud bang and the young woman's chest exploded right before Randy's eyes. She fell to the ground and it took a minute for Randy to regain his composure. When he looked to his left, he saw Yandy held the smoking gun. RiRi lay on the ground shaking when Randy kneeled beside her. Her eyes were as wide as they could get.

"I wasn't gonna shoot you," she mumbled as she struggled to breathe. A single tear escaped her eye followed by a deep breath. Then her eyes closed for the final time. Yandy heard a cell phone ringing and reached into RiRi's car to pull it out.

"Hello."

"Is it done?"

"Yeah, she's done," Yandy replied. "You'd better run far, you little bitch, 'cause you're next." She hung up.

## 26

R  andy was forced to resign as manager of the hotel and the
building was temporarily closed pending investigation of
the robbery. Afterward, Morgen was to take over as the
new manager which was his plan from the very beginning. Yandy
confessed to Randy that she kept four of the bags from the robbery.
Since Jenny didn't know how many there were, she couldn't
complain. Besides, it was enough money in those four bags to last
Jenny and her crew a lifetime. Randy was reluctant about checking
into rehab but he knew that it was the best thing for him. Yandy
packed him a bag then her and Polo drove him to the same center he
helped the mayor build.

"I can't believe you's a crackhead, man," Polo said from the driver's
seat.

Yandy nudged him then turned to face Randy. He was sitting low
in the back seat with dark shades on. "You okay, baby?" She questioned as she rubbed his knee.

"I'm fine. Still trying to get over the initial shock of all of this."

"Yeah. She pulled a good one, didn't she?" Yandy said with
admiration.

"Yes, she did," Randy admitted. "I'll catch up with her sooner or later. The world is not that big for her to hide from me."

"Remember, she's your daughter."

"Yeah, I created that monster." Polo pulled over in front of the rehab center, and Randy and Yandy stood outside the car eyeing each other.

"I'll be waiting when you return in six months," Yandy said. "Then we're gonna get married on some exotic island." She removed the old wedding band from his finger and tossed it.

"Thanks, Yandy," he said.

"There's only one way to thank me and that's by meeting me at the alter in your white tuxedo."

"White? Not black?" She shot him a look. "You got it," Randy said. When they hugged, he allowed real love to embrace him and it felt good. Polo sat his bags in front of him. They wanted to hug each other, but didn't know how to go about it.

"You know I fucked Jenny on your wedding night," Polo admitted.

"Dirty muthafucka."

"Couldn't help it. They gave me some of that same shit they gave you." Randy laughed and pulled Polo toward him.

"C'mere, man . . . Thank you."

"I'll be here when you get out."

"In a minute." Randy picked up his bags. "Don't fuck Yandy," he threw over his shoulder and Polo laughed. After Randy was shown around and settled into his new living quarters, they organized a special group session so everyone could introduce themselves. While the introductions were taking place, Randy zoned out. He thought about the caper that Yandy had pulled off. It was too bad that Spud and Chuck didn't make it. His friends left this earth before he could make amends. Tiffany got up under him then vanished with what she came for. It was a lesson learned. Randy had committed evil, and evil had returned to him.

The drug counselor called on Randy three times before he snapped out of his daze. He stood and adjusted his clothing. As he looked around the room at his fellow addicts of all ages and colors, he realized drugs could affect anyone no matter how young or powerful.

"Randy. Randy!" the voice called again. It was his conscience calling, and it was trying to tell him to wake up.

He took a deep breath and said, "Hi, my name is Randy Harris, and I'm a drug addict."

Polo parked in the garage of Morgen's downtown office, and he and Yandy took the emergency stairs to his floor. Morgen was on the phone, arguing with someone, when the door flew open. The henchman on the sofa reading the paper jumped up, but Polo fired two shots through the "Sports" section and watched as he crumpled to the floor. The phone fell from Morgen's hand as he rose from his seat, peering at Yandy who was walking toward him.

"Yandy?" he said as he backed up.

"Time for you to find out how long that jump is."

"No!" He grabbed the flagpole to use as a weapon. "Get back!" He swung it at Polo who dodged it then rushed Morgen, clutching his throat.

"Yo' fat ass tried to kill me," Polo said. "Didn't you know I did thirty years in the joint? Huh?"

"I'll pay you double whatever Randy is paying you. Please,"

Morgen pleaded. "Please!" Yandy threw his office chair through the window and the cold winter air blew in on them. "Please! Please!" Morgen begged. "Pleeeea—" The people walking below and driving on the street didn't know what to think when they saw Morgen come flying out the window. He hit the ground with a loud thump, as Yandy and Polo looked down on him.

"I'd say it's at least forty feet," Polo joked.

"At least," Yandy agreed. "Let's go."

*"Train a child the way he should go, and when he is old, he will not depart from it."*
*- Proverbs 22:6*